THE HAUNTED CIRCUS

THE HAUNTED CIRCUS

THOMAS McKEAN

SIMON & SCHUSTER BOOKS FOR YOUNG READERS

Published by Simon & Schuster
New York • London • Toronto • Sydney • Tokyo • Singapore

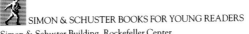 SIMON & SCHUSTER BOOKS FOR YOUNG READERS
Simon & Schuster Building, Rockefeller Center
1230 Avenue of the Americas, New York, New York 10020
Copyright © 1993 by Thomas McKean

SIMON & SCHUSTER BOOKS FOR YOUNG READERS
is a trademark of Simon & Schuster.

Designed by David Neuhaus
Manufactured in the United States of America   10 9 8 7 6 5 4 3 2 1

Library of Congress Cataloging-in-Publication Data
McKean, Thomas. The haunted circus/by Thomas McKean. Summary:
While staying with cousins at Bluebird Hall, twelve-year-old Edith is vis-
ited by a female ancestor from the early years of the century, who has
come forward in time to set Edith upon a quest for the young boy who will
become her grandfather. Sequel to "The Secret of the Seven Willows."
    [1. Time travel—Fiction.   2. Magic—Fiction.]   I. Title.
II. Series: McKean, Thomas.   Doors into time.
PZ7.M478658Hau   1993   [Fic]—dc20   92-32713 CIP
ISBN 0-671-72998-5

For Ruth Pitter

Contents

1

A COLD WIND FROM NOWHERE

"I can't believe this is happening to me," said Edith to herself as she put her hand on the doorknob. "Nothing's ever happened to me before, at least nothing like this."

It had all begun only a week before.

Edith's mother had to go away for three weeks, and Edith was to spend the time with her three cousins in Rock Ridge, Massachusetts. Their house, Bluebird Hall, had been in the Byram family since colonial times.

Edith hadn't been too happy about going. "I don't think Martha, Tad, and Joe like me very much," she'd complained. "And I don't think I like *them* very much, even if they are my cousins."

"Well, you can't stay here alone in New York City," her mother answered. "And you know how tight money has been since your father died; I couldn't possibly turn down this job. Besides, three weeks in the country will give you lots of time to write. You *do* have that story to finish for your new school. It's due soon, you know."

"I know," said Edith with a sigh of resignation.

At Bluebird Hall a similar discussion had taken place.

"No!" Martha Byram had said, tossing her head back so her long auburn hair went flying behind her. "Anything but that!"

"Now, now, dear," said Mrs. Byram, "it's only for three weeks."

"Good grief, Mom," said Tad, Martha's twin brother, "why did you tell Aunt Alida that Edith could stay with us? She's so . . . so . . ."

"Annoying," said Martha, finishing the sentence for Tad.

"Joe," said Mrs. Byram hopefully, "you're awfully quiet. Can you talk some sense into your brother and sister?"

Joe shook his head. He was the twins' older brother and liked setting a good example. But this time he sided with Tad and Martha.

"I'm sorry you feel this way," said Mrs. Byram. "Just try to remember how hard she and her mother have had it since Edith's father died."

Tad, Martha, and Joe had also lost their father only a few years before.

"Anyway," Mrs. Byram continued, "Tad, you can help your sister get Edith's room ready. Joe, would you help me with Aunt Alida's room? She'll be spending the night when she drops off Edith. And no monkey business!" she called after Tad and Martha as they headed upstairs.

"You know the worst of it," Martha fumed as soon as she and Tad were alone. "You're at science school all day, Joe's at sports camp, and I'm in drama school in Greenvale. We're not home till the late afternoon. And you know what *that* means," she added darkly.

2

"No time to explore," said Tad. "We'll never find magic again with Edith lurking around."

Bluebird Hall was more than just an old rambling house that had been in the Byram family since it was built back in the 1700s. Not too long ago, Tad, Martha, and Joe had discovered a magic ring in the field behind the house—and met a man named Tamburlaine Firshadow, who lived in a mysterious land at the border of time. After two journeys through time, they'd had to return the magic ring and the door through which they'd entered Tamburlaine's world had vanished forever. But Tamburlaine had told them that those who find magic once usually find it again. So, ever since then, the Byrams—especially Tad and Martha—had spent a lot of time looking for it. So far they had had no luck.

"Summer vacation seemed like the best time," said Martha.

"And now we'll have to spend three weeks of it with Edith Byram," said Tad. "And she doesn't even believe in magic."

"When we tried telling her, she wouldn't even listen," said Martha. "She didn't believe us. She said we were just making it all up. And she's such a goody-goody, too!"

"Why did Mom have to invite them?" moaned Tad.

"It's not fair," said Martha.

A tan Chevrolet inched up Bluebird Hall's long, tree-lined driveway. Every so often its brakes were slammed on and it came to a stop, only to continue its forward journey a moment or two later. At last it lurched to a final halt in front of Bluebird Hall. The stately white house seemed to be looking down in amusement.

"She can't even drive," said Martha.

It was Sunday afternoon, and the four Byrams were waiting by the front door.

Out of the driver's seat popped Aunt Alida. Neither Tad, Martha, nor Joe was especially fond of their aunt. They thought she was far too strict.

"Is there something wrong with your car?" asked Mrs. Byram.

"You kept lurching to a halt all the way up the drive," Martha pointed out.

"Oh, that," said Aunt Alida. "I was just testing the brakes. They've been known to fail after a long trip, and I didn't want to drive straight *into* Bluebird Hall, now did I? I *told* that mechanic to look into it, but likely he did not."

"Most wise, I'm sure," mumbled Mrs. Byram as the passenger door opened and out stepped Edith. She had bright blue eyes—Byram eyes, they were called in the family. They were her prettiest feature. Her light brown hair was pulled back in a long braid, accenting a large, pale forehead. She was tall, too—nearly as tall as Joe. But Joe was fourteen and Edith was twelve, a year older than Tad and Martha.

Edith was carrying a heavy book bag. As she exited the car, one of the bag's long straps tangled itself around her ankles and she fell with a thud onto the driveway.

Tad, Martha, and Joe looked away in embarrassment as Aunt Alida flew to her daughter's side.

"Careful with those books," admonished Aunt Alida as

she picked up a fallen volume, leaving Edith to dust herself off and get back on her feet. "Edith," said her mother a moment later, "you remember Tad, Martha, and Joe."

Edith examined her cousins. It was hard to tell Tad and Martha were twins. Tad was brown-eyed with sandy-colored hair, short for his age, and serious. Martha was tall and slim, with bright blue eyes, long auburn hair, and a very dramatic manner. She wanted to be an actress, Edith recalled, and usually acted like one. Edith didn't like her. Then there was Joe. He looked like Martha, with the same blue eyes—Byram eyes—but with blond hair. Edith thought he was handsome—far too handsome to bother with her.

Edith couldn't forget how her three cousins had tried to pull her leg with that incredible story. She was sure they'd just been teasing her. As soon as she acted as if she believed them, they would have started laughing at her. So Edith had refused to listen to them at all. Then they'd gotten mad at her.

"Martha," said Mrs. Byram, "won't you show Edith to her room? Boys, can you bring up the luggage?"

"Mom!" said Martha. "Girls can carry luggage, too. Joe can show Edith to her room. Tad and I will take care of the bags. C'mon, Tad."

"As you wish," sighed Mrs. Byram, ushering her sister-in-law into Bluebird Hall.

"Martha, Tad," called Mrs. Byram a little while later as Edith and her mother were unpacking. "I need you for a moment."

The twins soon arrived by their mother's side.

"What is it, Mom?"

"I just remembered that we put Edith in the little bedroom."

"Right," said Tad, "the room with no closet."

"That's just it," said Mrs. Byram. "There's a door there with only a wall behind it. There used to be a dressing room connecting two bedrooms, but your grandmother turned it into two storage closets with doors opening onto the hallway. Now, where can Edith hang her clothes?"

"How about out the window?" suggested Martha.

Mrs. Byram ignored that remark. "Could you please bring up that tall coatrack from the mudroom? And remind Edith about that door. She might open it without looking and walk smack into the wall! Aunt Alida worries so, and Edith *is* a bit, well . . ."

"Clumsy," said Martha. "And not just a bit."

"I was going to say absentminded," said Mrs. Byram quickly. "She is awfully intelligent. You know, I'll never know why they left that door there. Your father always said that your grandfather had a lively sense of humor. He even said it might come in handy someday. Imagine, a door that doesn't go anywhere! Anyway, now I've got to see about dinner."

"Listen," whispered Martha as soon as their mother had gone into the kitchen. "Let's forget the coatrack. I bet Edith will open the door and plow right into the plaster."

Upstairs in the far bedroom, Edith continued unpacking. She carefully put her blouses and smaller things into the bureau in the corner of the room. On the bed, ready to be hung in the closet, were some skirts, two pairs of corduroy pants, and a long raincoat.

With these items draped over her arm, Edith opened the door that once had led into a dressing room but now led nowhere at all. The light from her bedroom dimly lit a small, rectangular room.

Edith stepped in, looking for hangers, but the room was empty. Only blank walls stared back at her. A cold wind from nowhere was blowing through the room. It was strangely chilly, even stranger because it was a warm summer afternoon and the upstairs of the old house was a bit stuffy.

After some searching, Edith found a few hooks on the wall. She hung up her clothes as best she could. It took a while, and the chill of the empty room seemed to enter her bones—so much so, in fact, that when she came down for supper she was shivering slightly.

2

GHOSTS

After supper, Mrs. Byram gave Edith and her mother a tour of Bluebird Hall, showing off the recent renovations. Joe came along. He was especially proud of two family portraits they'd just had reframed. He also liked a photograph that Great-aunt Ruth had recently taken. It was a wonderful picture of Tad, Martha, and Joe. Great-aunt Ruth had printed an enlargement in her darkroom and framed it as a gift. Mrs. Byram had hung it only the day before.

"Mom!" cried Joe. "Look at the photograph!"

"Heavens!" said Mrs. Byram. "It's fading! And it was fine earlier today."

"We look like ghosts or something," said Joe in a low voice. " It gives me the creeps!"

"Hmmm," said Edith. "I'll bet Great-aunt Ruth just forgot to use the right chemicals or something. If you make that kind of mistake, a picture will fade."

"But look at us," said Joe, "Tad, Martha, and I are fading, but the meadow looks just the same."

Now it was Aunt Alida's turn to examine the photograph. "I think it only seems that way," she said.

"I'll just ask Ruth to print another copy," said Mrs. Byram. "Come on, Joe, let's show them the portraits."

"That's our grandfather, Timothy Byram," Joe announced, pointing to a painting of a serious-looking, blue-eyed man in his forties. Next to his portrait hung a painting of his sisters, Rosamond and Ruth. Ruth, now in her eighties, was the one who had taken the picture of the three Byram children. She was a retired painter who lived nearby in Greenvale.

"What a pity your grandfather died too soon for you children to know him," said Mrs. Byram. "Joe was only three and the twins were just born. His sister Rosamond died shortly after, some say of grief."

Edith looked at the portrait of her two great-aunts, done when both were in their forties. It showed two determined, lively-looking women. Edith knew her Great-aunt Ruth; she wished she'd known her other great-aunt, Rosamond.

"I can remember Grandfather Timothy," said Joe. Accidentally on purpose, Joe stood right next to his grandfather's portrait, adopting the same pose as Timothy Byram himself. He was hoping someone would mention what he thought was a striking resemblance.

Edith *was* just mentioning it while Tad and Martha were secretly investigating her room.

"No dent in the plaster," sighed Martha, opening the door that led nowhere.

"Maybe she didn't have time to finish all her unpacking," said Tad.

Martha's gaze swept around the small room. A row of books had already been placed on the windowsill.

"Alphabetical order even," Martha announced, shaking her head in disbelief. "What a bookworm."

Tad brushed his short hair back the way he did when he was trying to think of something to say. "I'm kind of a bookworm, too, you know."

"I know that," said Martha. "But you're fun, too. And a certain cousin isn't."

A certain cousin, however, was good at cards.

The six Byrams played a spirited game of hearts after dinner, and Edith won handily.

"I'm glad we weren't playing for money," said Joe. "Remind me *never* to play against Edith for money!"

"Edith won't have much time to play cards," put in Aunt Alida. "She has a great deal of writing to get done."

"I thought *I* had a good memory," said Tad to Martha as they were putting away the cardtable, "but Edith remembered every card that was put down."

"She is pretty sharp," admitted Martha. Then she gave a giggle. "Especially around the nose!"

Night settled in on Bluebird Hall.

Mrs. Byram was planning that week's menus, Joe was reading a sports magazine before turning in, and Tad and Martha were examining the basement inch by inch.

"I just feel it, down in my bones," announced Martha. "There is magic in the air."

"Good grief," said Tad. "There is nothing in *this* air but dust! Unless . . ."

"What?"

"Unless," continued Tad thoughtfully, "magic had something to do with that photograph fading."

"What a thought!" said Martha, peering behind a trunk.

Upstairs, Edith yawned, put down her book, and turned out the bedside lamp. It was such a warm July night that she was sleeping with only a light blanket.

Although Edith was tired, her mind kept working, as if by itself. If it's so warm, she was thinking, how can that walk-in closet be so cold? It doesn't make sense.

Edith decided to check out the room before going to sleep. She switched on her lamp and got out of bed. Shuffling along in her slippers, she entered the small room.

It was dark inside. The only light came from behind her. But the door into her bedroom had swung partially shut.

It was still chilly, perhaps a bit more so. Suddenly, soft light filtered in from the far side of the room.

Good, thought Edith, now I can see.

Then it struck her. On the room's far end, opposite her bedroom, a door had opened. The light was shining through the open door—a strange, blue light.

But there had been no door on that wall. Edith was sure of it.

In the doorway stood a girl. Her blue eyes were much like Edith's own. They had to be Byram eyes. The girl had long, dark hair—almost to her waist—tied back with blue ribbons that matched the color of her eyes.

Then Edith realized she could see right through the girl. Her cousins hadn't been teasing her after all.

"I need help," the girl said. "And since you have

11

come, then you are the one who will help me."

"What—" began Edith, but the girl continued speaking.

"Come closer," she said.

Edith took a step closer. From nowhere a bitter wind sprung up in the dark room.

At the same moment a loud knocking on her bedroom door shattered the quiet. "Edith! Edith!" called an insistent voice.

"My mother," explained Edith. "She's always . . ."

The transparent girl headed back through the mysterious door. As she moved, she started fading. Before vanishing completely, she spoke once more. "I will try again tomorrow. But if that fails, then all is lost—for me, and for you."

When the girl disappeared, Edith raced from the room, closing the door behind her. She opened her bedroom door and let in her mother.

"Just checking, dear," said Edith's mother. "Were you reading? Please, don't be too distracted by your cousins, and work as hard at your writing as you can."

"I will, Mom, I will."

"Glad to hear it," said Aunt Alida before heading off down the long hallway, leaving Edith still trying to make sense of what had happened.

In the morning, Edith was half convinced that the transparent girl had been a dream. She checked out the little room but found no door on the far wall.

On the way down to breakfast, Edith examined the

hallway. Right next to her room, opening onto the hall-way, were two large closets: one for linen, one for brooms and cleaning supplies. Edith saw at a glance that the size of the two closets equaled that of the little room. Then she realized that the two closets were in the exact same place as the little room.

But that was *impossible*.

Edith returned to her bedroom. There was the little room, and it *was* in exactly the same place as the two clos-ets. One of its walls ran along the outside of Bluebird Hall, the other wall faced the hallway. Edith even paced out the space. The small room was about twelve-by-eight steps in measurement. So were the closets.

She then checked out the room just beyond the closets. It was in the northeast corner of Bluebird Hall and was only a junk room. But there was a door on one wall. This had to be the door that the transparent girl had opened the night before—the door that wasn't there this morning.

Edith took a deep breath and flung open the door.

"It's just like the one in your room," said a voice behind her.

Edith wheeled around. There stood her aunt.

"It's curious, isn't it," Mrs. Byram continued, "having two doors leading nowhere at all. But, you see, there used to be a little room right between your room and this one. It was converted into those two hall closets. I've often wondered why the doors were left there at all. It's always a surprise to open them and find nothing but white plaster wall. I've wanted to lock them permanently since they don't go anywhere, but the keys are lost and it doesn't seem worthwhile having new ones made. Now, the strap on your mother's suitcase broke, and I said I'd lend her one of mine. I know it's somewhere in all this junk."

"Aunt Margaret," said Edith, "you mean that the door in my room is like this one? It doesn't go anywhere?"

"Odd, isn't it," said Mrs. Byram. "Ah, there's the suitcase. See you at breakfast."

Once again Edith was left alone to wonder.

"And furthermore," Edith's mother was telling Mrs. Byram over breakfast, "Edith must spend three hours each morning and two hours each afternoon at her writing. She has to write a story that will determine which English class she'll be in next year. It's important."

"Isn't five hours a day rather a lot?" asked Mrs. Byram while Tad, Martha, and Joe eyed Edith with a bit more sympathy. Their mother would never make them work alone in their rooms for so long, especially during the summer.

"Five hours a lot?" said Aunt Alida, repeating the question. "Of course not. Edith must get used to hard work if she's to do well at her new school."

Edith, meanwhile, seemed oblivious to the discussion. She had a faraway look in her eyes. She was longing to tell her cousins about her discovery, but she was too embarrassed. She hadn't believed them when they'd told her, and they'd been right. Magic did exist—it had to! But if she told her cousins, she'd have to admit that she'd been wrong, and like most people, Edith hated admitting she was wrong. And something told her that Martha wouldn't make it easy for her, either.

No wonder her mother walks all over her, thought Martha critically. She doesn't even put up an argument. She's just sitting there!

Joe, too, was examining Edith's expression. There was something familiar about it. That was it! It was the way Tad and Martha had looked when they'd found Tamburlaine's world, but before they'd told him about it. But Edith? Joe put the thought out of his mind and concentrated on his toast.

Aunt Alida and her tan Chevrolet had soon vanished down Bluebird Hall's long driveway, with Tad, Martha, and Joe crammed into the backseat. Their aunt was going to drop them in Rock Ridge. From there they could either walk or take a bus to their various destinations.

Mrs. Byram was clearing away the breakfast dishes when Edith saw it. It was sitting on a table in the living room. Edith looked at it carefully. No, there was no doubt about it. The shock caused her to give a quick cry of surprise.

"Anything the matter?" called Mrs. Byram from the sink.

"It's . . . it's this little portrait," replied Edith. "This one of the two children reading a book with a man standing behind them. Who are they?"

"Come help me get the plates washed, then I'll tell you what I can," came the answer.

Soon Edith and her aunt were seated together on

the sofa, the small portrait in Edith's hand.

"It was your Great-aunt Ruth who found this," explained Mrs. Byram. "I'm not sure where she got it. She just came across it recently."

"But who's the girl?" asked Edith, for the girl in the portrait was the girl she'd seen in the room that wasn't there.

"Why, that's your Great-aunt Rosamond when she was a girl. This is the same person you saw in the portrait last night. And the boy is her twin brother, Timothy. Your grandfather, of course. Who the man behind them is, I couldn't say. I have the feeling that Ruth knows, but I can't get her to tell. I even get the feeling that Tad, Martha, and Joe know more about him than they'll say."

Yes, it was the girl in the room. And the boy next to her—Edith's grandfather—looked remarkably like Joe. Edith turned her attention to the man standing behind them. He had an out-of-doors look, with blue-green eyes and shiny black hair. And he had a very mysterious air about him.

Edith's thoughts were interrupted by her aunt.

"I must get to work," she said. "I've started doing some private consulting work, and I've got a lot to do. So do you. I'm sorry, Edith, but I did promise your mother that you'd write for three hours each morning, so it's up to your room, I'm afraid."

But Edith didn't mind being sent to her room. She knew what was waiting there.

3

LOST

This time when Edith opened the door to the little room, it was utterly dark. Stepping inside, she was suddenly aware of a cold, howling wind blowing through the dark room. It was moaning and crying, like something in pain — or grief.

Then four dim lines of blue light appeared on the far wall. They formed a rectangular shape. Edith realized it was the outline of a door, with light coming from somewhere behind it. The light grew brighter as the door was opened. A girl stepped through the door, her hair tied back with long ribbons, her eyes flashing. She was still transparent. Edith imagined that she could almost see the wind blowing through her.

The girl walked straight toward Edith, her left arm raised. In her hand she held an old-fashioned lantern. Though the candle was behind glass, its small flame was buffeted by the wind.

Edith approached the girl. "I was right," she said softly. "You are Rosamond."

The two girls looked at one another.

"But it's impossible!" cried Edith. "You're not much older than I am, but you're my grandfather's twin sister."

"I am fifteen," said Rosamond. Then she gestured behind her. "You see that door?" she asked. "Not long ago I found it, and this room, a room that doesn't exist in my time. I had gone through a crawl space that Timothy and I used to play in. And I found something. It was this door. I went through it," continued Rosamond, as the bitter wind whipped her long hair around her face, "and came into this room. A man was there. He told me to return to this room if I truly needed help. He said help would come—someone would find me."

"But I just came through an old closet door," protested Edith.

"Whenever anyone else opens that closet door, they see a blank wall of plaster," said Rosamond. "For you it is different."

"Once when Timothy and I were playing in the crawl space," Rosamond continued in a dreamy voice, "he fell. The doctor had to come and stitch up his elbow. The scar is still there, I am sure. Not that I have seen it, of course, not since we lost Timothy."

"Lost Timothy? What happened to him?"

"No one knows," sighed Rosamond, and it seemed as though the wind had died down to listen. "At least, Mother and Father believe him dead. It was back in 1912, just before our fourth birthday. Our younger sister, Ruth, was only a baby. Anyway, soon after they painted the portrait you saw, there was a terrible epidemic and Timothy took ill, very ill. He was coughing and had a frightfully high fever. Mother was beside herself. The doctor came, and he said that Timothy was too sick to be treated locally. There was no hospital in Rock Ridge in those days. Well, they took Timothy to a hospital in Boston, along with some others from the village who had become seriously ill, too. Mother was not permitted to go. It was a horse-drawn wagon, you see, and there was no room for relatives. So Timothy had to go alone. Boston seemed very distant. I remember crying as the wagon rolled down the drive. Weeks went by. Then word came."

Rosamond looked troubled. The more troubled she looked, the more the wind started blowing again. It became fiercer and fiercer. Edith was sure it would blow out the lantern any second.

"They wrote us," said Rosamond, "that Timothy had died, and that, to avoid further infection, he had been buried in a mass grave near Boston. Mother cried for weeks."

"Oh, but that's terrible," said Edith.

"Yes, it was. Very terrible. Because, you see, it was not true."

"How do you know . . ." began Edith, then stopped as a thought struck her. "But he couldn't have died!" she cried. "He's my grandfather! His portrait is downstairs! If he'd died when he was four, then . . ."

"Then you wouldn't be here," said Rosamond bluntly.

"You see," she continued, "Timothy is my twin. I don't care what anyone says. I *know* he's alive somewhere. I know a mistake has been made. But no one believes me. Except Tamburlaine."

"Tamburlaine?"

"Tamburlaine Firshadow. He's, well, no one can quite explain what he is. Anyway, he told me I was right: My brother is still alive. And he must be brought back to Bluebird Hall. Tamburlaine said that whoever found his or her way to this room would be the one who could help me. And I'm glad it's you. After all, we're both twins."

Edith's heart leapt into her throat. So, she thought, all this isn't even meant for me. It's meant for Martha. *She* is the twin. Edith felt Rosamond looking at her intently.

"Whatever is the matter?" asked Rosamond.

For a moment Edith considered not telling Rosamond who she really was. Then she knew she had to. "I'm not Martha," she said. "I'm Edith. Her cousin."

"Not Martha?" echoed Rosamond, stunned. "Not the girl I'd heard about, the one who lives in Bluebird Hall?"

"I could get her," offered Edith unhappily.

"No," said Rosamond with resolution—and, thought Edith, some sorrow. "You are the one who found this room. It must be you. Besides, there isn't time."

"What do you mean, there isn't time?"

"Every second I am away from my own time, it becomes harder to stay here. It's as though some immense magnet were pulling me back. That's why I'm transparent, I'm only partly here. I can't stay much longer."

"But can't you come back?" Edith asked.

"This is my third and last trip," said Rosamond. "I can't return until you do it."

"Do *it!*" cried Edith as the wind started rising in the dark room. "Do *what?*"

"Find Timothy for me, and bring him back to Bluebird Hall."

"But I wouldn't even know where to start. And besides, I'm just not very good at this kind of thing. I mean, I'm good at school stuff, not finding things."

"You found the room that wasn't there," said Rosamond as the wind howled louder.

"But—"

"There is no time for questions. But I must tell you one thing: The man I spoke of, Tamburlaine Firshadow, he will help you."

"How do I find him?" asked Edith.

"Look for his door," called Rosamond over the rising wind. "It will appear. It has to."

I can't do this, Edith was thinking as the wind tore at her hair. I'd go out and find nobody, or else I'd find the wrong person, or else—I don't even know. I just know I can't do it.

"Will you do it?" repeated Rosamond, fixing Edith with her luminous eyes.

Edith was shivering so much she could barely speak. She meant to say "no," but somehow something else came out. "Yes," said Edith's voice. "Yes."

At the word "yes" the wind dropped for an instant, as though it were making sure of Edith's response. Then it seemed to gather all its strength. An icy blast hit both

Edith and Rosamond. The force of it knocked Edith to the floor. Looking up, she saw another gust send Rosamond flying across the narrow room as though she were merely a paper doll. When Rosamond reached the far wall, she disappeared altogether.

Had she made it through the door to her own time, Edith wondered, or had the wind just blown her into nothingness? On hands and knees, Edith crawled out of the room that wasn't there, out of the wind and the darkness, back into the warmth of her room in Bluebird Hall.

LIFELINES

Edith lay on the floor of her room, a storm-tossed bird who had found its nest at last. Then she thought of Rosamond. "I hope you're all right," she said in a half-whisper through the still-open door.

"You hope I'm all right?" said a puzzled voice.

Edith looked up from the floor. There stood her aunt, a worried look clouding her kind face.

"Edith," she said, "I was just passing by. I didn't mean to spy. But are you all right? What are you doing there on the floor, talking to a blank wall?"

"A blank wall?" said Edith. Then she realized that her aunt couldn't see the dark room.

Edith clambered to her feet. "I was just doing some . . . exercises. You have to do them on the floor."

"Sounds interesting," said Mrs. Byram, wondering why Edith's hair looked as if she'd been out in a hurricane. And why was she so flushed?

Hmmm, she thought, heading down the hall. Perhaps

Edith is more like her cousins than she seems.

"Where's Edith?" asked Martha when she got home from drama class.

"In her room, writing," replied Mrs. Byram, looking up from her work. "Let her do her schoolwork, darling. Don't disturb her, please."

"I wouldn't dream of it," said Martha, heading straight for Edith's room. Imagine staying inside on such a beautiful day, Martha was thinking. *I* would never be caught dead doing that!

But a quick inspection proved Edith's room to be empty.

Good for her, thought Martha. She's got some spunk, at least. I wonder where she went.

Had Martha but known it, Edith was with an old friend of hers, and probably the one person on earth that she, Tad, and Joe most wished to see again.

It had happened right after lunch.

Mrs. Byram still thought Edith looked flushed and over-excited. I never knew writing was so exhilarating, she mused, watching Edith down her lunch rapidly. It looks as though she can't wait to get back to her room and start writing again.

When the last of the egg salad was gone, Edith made a beeline for her room. Nervous as she was, Edith couldn't remember ever being quite so excited about anything.

She had spent the morning checking the little room every five minutes to see if Tamburlaine's door had appeared. Yet so far, nothing. Tamburlaine. She already liked the sound of his name.

Now, saying Tamburlaine's name again for good luck, Edith pushed open the door and looked in hopefully.

The room was as empty as ever, except for a playful wind that rustled softly.

Edith was about to shut the door when the wind suddenly increased its strength. She stepped into the room and, just as she did, the force of the wind slammed the bedroom door behind her.

Edith stared, for there on the dark room's outside wall, a door was appearing. At first it was just a misty form, then a golden glow. At last it solidified into an old-fashioned door. It was made of shining, perfectly polished wood. On it was a small plaque engraved with two words: Tamburlaine Firshadow.

Edith summoned her courage and approached the gleaming door.

Before she could even knock, the door opened.

A man with remarkable blue-green eyes and shiny black hair ushered her in. Edith recognized him immediately: He was the man in the portrait standing behind the children.

Edith found herself in a log cabin in the middle of wild country. A comfortable-looking sofa and a wooden rocking chair stood on a braided rug in front of a large stone fireplace with a fire burning in it.

A fox was curled up on the rocking chair, a white owl was perched on the man's shoulder. Both the man and the owl were gazing into Edith's eyes, looking right through her, Edith felt.

"I'm not Martha," she blurted out. "I'm not the one you thought I'd be."

The man gave a smile. Then he spoke. "Edith," he said, "welcome. It is all as it was meant to be. Come find a seat by the fire. We shall have some tea, and talk."

Edith and the man sat on the sofa, warming themselves by the fire.

"I don't understand," said Edith. "The view out your window isn't the view from Bluebird Hall. There's a field with seven willows."

"You are no longer in Bluebird Hall," Tamburlaine explained. "You are the first person to find the way to the room. And that means that you have much to do, and very little time to do it. You must return Timothy Byram to Bluebird Hall—and to his proper path in life. His loss was a mistake, a mistake that must be righted."

"But how can I?" burst out Edith. "He died years ago."

"He is *alive*," said Tamburlaine simply and with such conviction that it was impossible to doubt him.

"But if he's alive, why doesn't he just come back to Bluebird Hall?"

"I imagine he has forgotten who he is. After all, he was taken away when he was not yet even four years old, and extremely ill, too," said Tamburlaine. "He must be *brought* back."

"But if he's my grandfather," said Edith, "how could he *not* come back. I mean, if he didn't, then I wouldn't be here. Neither would Joe, Tad, or Martha."

Tamburlaine gave a sad smile. "I shall try to explain," he said. "People can lead parallel lives, their own destined life as well as an alternate one when their destiny has gone off course." Picking up a long piece of string, he looped it around one finger of his left hand and held up the two ends with his right so that they formed a long U. "Time," he said, "is not as simple as we like to think. There are many different times. Sometimes they even run side by side. Sometimes they form gigantic loops. Sometimes one can journey from one time to another. There are even some places beyond time."

"Like the room that isn't there?" said Edith.

"Correct," said Tamburlaine. "Sometimes it is all right for timelines to run side by side. Perhaps even necessary. But at other times they are meant to be intertwined. So it is with your lifeline and the lifeline of Timothy Byram. They were meant to be intertwined. Like this."

Deftly, Tamburlaine twirled one of his long fingers so both sides of the string were wrapped around each other.

"But what happens if Timothy isn't brought back?"

Tamburlaine looked grave. "I would rather not say too much about that," he replied. "Let me just say that not only does *his* life depend on you finding him, but yours depends on it, too. Your lifelines must be entwined."

Edith tried hard to put what seemed impossible into words. "You mean that if I don't return Timothy Byram to his proper path, then I might . . . just vanish? Like Tad, Martha, and Joe in that photograph?"

"Possibly," said Tamburlaine. "Or perhaps other sorrows might occur. As it is now, your existence, as well as your cousins', is based on an event that never happened. It could be that your life—and the lives of your father and uncle and cousins—are but reflections of what was meant to be."

"But what if I find Timothy and he's an old man?"

27

Tamburlaine smiled again.

"All you need do, Edith, is bring Timothy home, no matter how old he is when you find him. Once he is found and brought to the room, I can do the rest. It is for the moment but a step from that room to my world, but it will not always be so. Once Timothy enters my world, I can return him to the past and to the age he should be. But he must be found first, and that is something I cannot do. I must stay where I am—beyond the past, outside the present."

"Do we have so little time because of Timothy's age?" asked Edith.

"Yes," replied Tamburlaine. "He must not die in his other life before he can be brought home. If he dies there, too, it will be too late."

"But couldn't Rosamond go to find him?" asked Edith, suddenly afraid. "He's her brother. And did she . . ."

"Yes," said Tamburlaine to Edith's unasked question. "Rosamond did make it back to her own time. And there she must stay—an anchor for Timothy to return to. She cannot make the voyage to find him. Only you can."

"But Aunt Margaret would never let me go off looking for some old man, not even if he is my grandfather."

"There are ways," said Tamburlaine with a smile. He then clapped his strong hands together. As if obeying a command, the owl flew from his shoulder and out of the window of the cabin. Minutes later, with a hoot and a rush of wind, she returned. She was carrying a ring in her talons.

"She has flown farther in what to you felt but a few

minutes than most people travel in a lifetime," said Tamburlaine.

The owl deposited the ring in Tamburlaine's open palm and resumed her place on his shoulder.

"My father made this ring," said Tamburlaine. "Once it was two separate rings. Long, long ago they were combined into one and invested with a powerful magic. But, not too long ago, that ring was lost on the far frontiers of my land, where time zones have their shifting borders. It is a dangerous place, under no one's control. Then, recently, for reasons of its own, the ring returned to me. Its magic is still strong, but different than before. I believe it somehow knew it would be needed to locate Timothy. Because, you see, at the same time it returned, Rosamond was able to enter the room that isn't there."

"What exactly *is* the room?"

"In some ways," Tamburlaine said, "it is like a bubble outside the current of time, a bubble connecting different times—yours, mine, and Rosamund's. While it is here, one can go from one time to another. But much like a bubble, it cannot last long."

"But where did the room come from?"

"Maybe it simply created itself," Tamburlaine said, "and then called to you. Or perhaps the ring helped create it."

"The ring could do that?"

"That and more," said Tamburlaine. "Once, when it was first made, this ring gave but one wish. Now it can assist in many. And it can work through both time and space, and perhaps more. I do not yet know all."

For the first time, Edith noticed Tamburlaine was wearing a ring nearly identical to the one he was holding.

"Perhaps," he said, "if you agree, we shall learn more about what this ring can and cannot do."

"Agree?" said Edith.

"I mean," said Tamburlaine, "agree to locate Timothy, by searching for him in the past and finding out where he has gone and what he has become."

"I still don't get it," Edith had to admit. "Are you going to send me up in a rocket or something?" she asked, her pale forehead getting paler.

"Nothing so dramatic," said Tamburlaine. "With this ring on one's finger, one can make a door into time appear. Once you pass through the door, you enter a different world."

"I don't believe it," Edith burst out. "It's impossible!"

"So are many of the things you have seen lately," said Tamburlaine. "Let me show you."

Tamburlaine put the ring on his finger. It was almost the color of silver, and Edith noticed a faint design of interlocking loops. Once the ring was on, Tamburlaine bowed his head in deep concentration. At last he raised his head and looked at the wall beyond him.

Edith looked, too.

The wall was made of rough logs, laid horizontally. As Edith watched, the grain of the wood seemed to come to life. It began changing direction until some of it was running vertically. Then, slowly, it turned into a flat, gray door.

Tamburlaine rose and opened the door. He placed the

ring on one of the owl's mighty talons. The owl then flew through the door and vanished.

The next second the owl reappeared. She was holding something. It was a stuffed animal.

"Teddy!" cried Edith, leaping to her feet to grab a worn-out old teddy bear.

Edith rocked the toy in her arms, smiling happily. "My father gave him to me," she said. Then the smile faded from her lips. "But," she began, "this can't be! Teddy was dropped down my apartment building's incinerator shaft by mistake. He was all burned up. I was only six. I cried for days."

"So he was," said Tamburlaine. "But I sent the owl back to *before* that happened."

"So it *is* all possible," said Edith. "It really is."

Tamburlaine smiled gently as Edith rocked the long-lost toy. "You may keep Teddy," he told her. "Generally, however, you must try to change the past as little as possible. You must only do what must be done—nothing more. And nothing less."

"But how will I know what must be done?"

"You will know," Tamburlaine said simply. "One word of warning: Your aim may not be perfect. Time will tell. And one other thing. Once you pass through the door, you must remove the ring, putting it on again only when you wish to return. The voyage home, you see, is the easier one. Any door will do, as long as you are wearing the ring. You are returning to your proper place in time and space. Your having left it creates sort of a vacuum that can only be filled by your return."

31

"So," said Edith, her mind working rapidly, "how do we start?"

"What do you suggest?" inquired Tamburlaine.

"I know!" exclaimed Edith, so excited that she rose to her feet. "I know! We'll start by going to the hospital where Timothy was sent in 1912. We do know the name of the hospital, don't we?"

"Yes," said Tamburlaine, "Rosamond told me the name."

"Do we start right now?" Edith asked next.

"Tomorrow," said Tamburlaine, handing Edith the ring. "Tomorrow will be time enough. Take good care of the ring, Edith," he added, "and it will take good care of you."

5

THE FIRST VOYAGE

Tad, Martha, and Joe were searching the big field behind Bluebird Hall. That was where they'd first found Tamburlaine's ring, and they were hoping magic would strike there again.

Mrs. Byram was watching them from the living room window. Dinner was over, the dishes were washed, and Tad, Martha, and Joe had fairly darted from the kitchen. They hadn't even invited Edith along with them.

"They look as though they've lost something," murmured Mrs. Byram.

Edith was just considering whether or not to tell her aunt about her discovery when she recalled her aunt hadn't been able to see the room that wasn't there. Edith longed to tell her cousins, but she was still too proud to admit she'd been wrong in not believing them.

I'll go all by myself this once, then I'll tell them, Edith resolved. So even if they are still angry with me, at least they'll be impressed with my being brave enough to go all by myself.

Edith looked out at her cousins, so busy in the field, and

pitied them a bit. She was on the verge of traveling through time, and there they were, looking for something in the grass.

The three Byrams were also pitying Edith.

"Dull," pronounced Martha. "Dull, dull, dull. All she does is study."

"She even alphabetized her books," put in Tad. He felt secretly guilty about saying this because he, too, kept his books in alphabetical order.

"I can't put my finger on it," said Joe after a pause, "but there's something about her—something unusual."

"Her nose," said Martha.

"Give it a rest, Martha," Joe shot back. "I think maybe we've been wrong about her."

"I think maybe we've been wrong about looking in this field," said Tad, giving the ground a kick. "Martha said there was magic in the air, but I don't think it's in this field."

"It's not just to look for magic that I wanted to come here," said Joe in a low voice.

"Then what is it?" demanded Martha.

Joe cleared his throat and told them about the fading photograph.

"I agree with Edith," said Tad. "I bet Great-aunt Ruth simply forgot to finish it correctly. After all, she *is* pretty old, and developing pictures is fairly complicated."

"I thought so, too, at first," replied Joe. "But that's not all. There's something else. When I took the picture out of the frame to get a better look, well, I got the chills. I felt cold all over, just like something awful was about to happen."

"Maybe you're catching a cold," suggested Martha.

"No," said Joe, "it felt like magic."

"Possibly," said Tad. "But there's just one way to find out for sure. We'll drop by Great-aunt Ruth's and ask her to print another picture. Then we'll see if that one fades."

"But what if it does?" cried Martha, suddenly worried.

"One thing at a time," said Tad. "Our first stop is Great-aunt Ruth's. We'll go there tomorrow after our classes."

Tomorrow came, and while Tad, Martha, and Joe were making plans to meet at their great-aunt's house in Greenvale, which was next to Rock Ridge, Edith was standing in the center of the small, dark room, gathering her thoughts. Surely Tamburlaine hadn't meant for her to leave all alone, without even saying good-bye.

Edith looked hopefully toward the outer wall, where she'd last seen Tamburlaine's door. But the wall was blank. It even seemed to be staring back at Edith, mocking her hope.

It seemed that the harder she tried to think of the name of Timothy's hospital, the harder the wind blew through the room—a cold, biting wind, almost an angry one. Edith couldn't decide if the wind was trying to help her, whistling and moaning and interrupting her thoughts.

"Oh, Tamburlaine," said Edith, half to herself, "make this wind stop blowing so I can think!"

"There is no net to catch the wind," said a low, musical voice, "especially the wind of time, for it blows where it will."

Edith wheeled around.

"Tamburlaine!" she cried, seeing the calm stranger

standing behind her. "I thought I'd have to leave without saying good-bye to anyone!"

"I would not have let you leave like that," said Tamburlaine softly. "And besides, there are a few things yet for you to learn."

As Tamburlaine began speaking, the wind calmed.

"First," he said, "as you know, you are going to Boston in the year 1912, to the Vine Street Hospital. Timothy will be but a child. You must make sure that he trusts you. Then you can tell him who he is and bring him back with you. Just make sure the ring is on, and that you are holding both his hands. You must surround him so he is enveloped in the power of the ring."

"Is it all right if I bring some stuff with me? I put it in a knapsack. I even packed a camera."

"You may bring whatever you wish."

"Is it time to start now?" asked Edith.

Tamburlaine nodded, so Edith put on the ring.

A shiver passed through her as the ring slid on her finger.

"The magic begins," said Tamburlaine simply. "Now you must concentrate, to call up the door into time."

Edith bowed her head. At first nothing happened.

Edith redoubled her efforts. She opened her eyes to check.

Yes! Glimmering in the dark, the door was waiting for her.

"Remember," said Tamburlaine, "once you pass through, take off the ring. Only put it back on when you are ready to return."

Edith said a silent prayer and pulled gently at the door-knob.

Nothing happened.

She pulled harder. And harder.

Still nothing happened. The door wouldn't open.

Tamburlaine, meanwhile, was watching with a gentle smile.

"I think," he said, "that you have to push this door. And now, I shall wish you a good voyage. It is time to go."

Edith paused, her hand resting on the doorknob. Her knees felt like Jell-O, and her heart was thumping in her throat.

"Go in peace," said Tamburlaine, "and return in peace."

Edith took a deep breath, summoning all her courage. She opened the door wide and stepped through.

For a moment, she thought she saw the lawn of Blue-bird Hall stretching out beneath her. Then the summer greenness vanished into a bright whiteness.

It lasted only a few seconds, yet it seemed like hours. Edith felt as though she were moving rapidly through space—rising and falling at the same time, seeing stars forming and exploding, watching clouds of light massing and swirling all around her.

Then it was over. She felt solid ground beneath her feet.

For a moment, Edith was too scared to look around. Before she even opened her eyes, she removed the ring and placed it carefully in a buttoned pocket.

She just caught a glimpse of a long, dark, institutional

hallway when a crisp voice spoke. "My, young lady, how you startled me! You seemed to simply pop in from nowhere."

Wheeling around awkwardly, Edith saw a plump woman in white, standing behind a wooden counter. A pretty lamp with a green shade cast a calm light, and an old-fashioned pen lay across some sheets of paper. Edith looked more carefully and saw the woman was wearing the white uniform of a nurse.

"I'm looking for Timothy Byram," burst out Edith.

"It is eleven o'clock in the evening," replied the nurse. "Visiting hours were over long ago. I cannot even imagine how you made it past the guards."

"I've come a long way," said Edith. "I mean, a *really* long way. I just got here. And I've got to see Timothy Byram. He's my grand—, I mean, he's . . . he's not feeling grand. That's it. Not grand at all."

Now it was the nurse's turn to examine Edith.

"Young lady," she said, eyeing Edith's corduroy pants, "your attire is most inappropriate for a hospital visit—or for anywhere, for that matter. A proper young lady wears a modest skirt at all times."

"Oh," said Edith, looking around. She noted that the passing nurses all wore skirts down to their ankles. "Sorry. I forgot how different things used to be."

"I beg your pardon?"

"I mean, I forgot to change. You see, I just leapt on my horse when I heard my grand—, I mean, my cousin was ill and didn't stop until I got to Boston."

"I couldn't possibly let you see him tonight," said the nurse. "But you know, dear, I ride, too. I shall look up his chart and tell you how he is doing. Now, what was his name?"

"No," said the nurse a few moments later. "I have gone over the roster three times, and there is no one by the name of Timothy Byram."

"But there has to be," said Edith. "I know for a fact he was brought here, very ill and suffering from a high fever, in September 1912."

The nurse dropped the roster she'd been consulting. A worried look appeared on her face and she peered at Edith nervously. "Did you say 1912?" she asked.

"Yes, I did," replied Edith.

The nurse shook her head before speaking. "You are ten years too late," she said.

"What do you mean?" demanded Edith. "You mean he was brought here in 1902? But he wasn't even born then!"

"No, I do not mean he was brought here in 1902. I mean that the year is 1922."

"You mean it's not 1912?" asked Edith.

"That is exactly what I mean."

"Darn! I'm in the wrong year."

Once again the nurse eyed Edith warily. "Perhaps we are overtired from our trip," she said, trying to sound sweet. "Perhaps we should sit for a minute or two."

She was saying we, but she clearly meant Edith. And there was something in her tone Edith didn't quite trust.

"Here is a chair, dear," the nurse continued. "I shall return in just a moment. I must check on something."

Leaving Edith on an uncomfortable wooden chair, she scuttled quickly down the hallway.

After a second's hesitation, Edith followed.

If she happens to turn around and see me, thought Edith, I can always say I was scared of being left alone.

But the nurse was too intent on whatever it was she was doing to even look back.

Edith shadowed her to a room down the corridor. Pausing outside the door, Edith eavesdropped.

"Yes, Nurse Waldo. What is it?" inquired a grumpy voice.

"Excuse me, doctor, but there is a most peculiar girl by the desk."

"So? There are plenty of peculiar people in Boston."

"Excuse me, doctor, but I think she must have escaped from some lunatic asylum. She didn't even know what year it was."

"Really," said the doctor. "I shall see to her in a moment. Now, Nurse Waldo, I have to . . ."

Edith didn't wait to hear what it was that needed doing.

If I don't get out of here, she thought, running down the corridor, they'll put me in an insane asylum.

Edith was about to put the ring back on when a thought occurred to her. It's not really stealing, she told herself. It's more like borrowing.

Edith leaned over the front desk and riffled through the various rosters that were neatly shelved there. They were divided by year and season. At last she found what she was looking for: 1912.

Putting the book under her arm, Edith ran down the corridor, away from the room in which the nurse and doctor were working. She raced down a marble staircase and out into the streets of Boston in the year 1922.

BRIAN THOMAS

"No," Great-aunt Ruth was saying, "I am sure I developed that picture properly, quite sure."

Great-aunt Ruth's blue eyes blazed dramatically in her almost wrinkle-free face. Despite being in her eighties, Great-aunt Ruth remained one of the most stimulating people the Byrams knew. She had done many things in her life but was best known for her painting. More recently she had returned to her old hobby of photography.

"But just look at it," said Tad, producing the photograph. "We're fading away completely."

"We're more faded now than we were yesterday," added Joe. "A lot more."

"Yet the grass around us looks just the same," put in Martha.

Great-aunt Ruth looked troubled. "This could be serious," she said, half to herself. "It reminds me of . . ." she began, then paused. "No," she said in her normal voice, "it might not be that at all. Perhaps there *is* a logical explanation. Perhaps I *did* overlook some part of the developing process."

"Why don't you just make another print," suggested Tad. "I'm sure it won't happen again."

"I hope not, I do hope not," murmured Ruth. "At any rate," she continued, brightening, "I have a little surprise for you. In fact, it was rather a surprise for me, I must say."

"I adore surprises," said Martha.

"While I was working in my darkroom, I came across an old box I had quite forgotten about. It was filled with all sorts of odds and ends. But there was one treasure. I found a negative of the very first photograph I ever took, back when I was a girl. I developed it and made a copy for you three. I thought that you might enjoy seeing the way things looked when I was young."

Soon Tad, Martha, and Joe were pouring over a sepia-tinted photograph. It had been taken at a traveling circus and showed a crowd of people in old-fashioned clothing gathered around a ticket seller's booth.

"I recall my father suggesting that it might be a good subject for a photograph," said Ruth.

"Look!" cried Martha. "Back then the circus only cost five cents."

Tad was examining the picture closely. "Good grief!" he said. "You even caught a small poster next to the booth, listing that night's acts. Let's see. It says, New Additions. The White Wonder and Brian Thomas, the Colorado Cowboy."

"I wonder what the White Wonder was," said Joe.

"I'm afraid I never got to actually see the show," said

Ruth. "But I did get to meet many of the performers," she added with a faraway smile. "Some of them even came to Bluebird Hall. Oh, well, that was a long time ago."

"Hey, look at this fat lady over in the corner!" exclaimed Martha. "She's gigantic!"

"And this looks like a bearded lady!" cried Tad.

In their excitement over the photo of the circus, they forgot their worry about the fading photograph of themselves.

"Wow," said Tad, "there sure is a lot going on in this picture."

"Yes," said Great-aunt Ruth, "and I think the more you look, the more you'll find."

It happened on the bus ride home from their great-aunt's. Tad, Martha, and Joe were crammed into a double seat.

"Did you get the feeling," Tad was saying, "that Great-aunt Ruth knew much more than she was telling us?"

"I thought so, too," said Joe. "I thought she was really worried about that picture fading."

"Maybe she just felt bad about having made a mistake in printing it," suggested Martha.

"Maybe," said Tad. "*If* she actually made a mistake, that is."

"But she must have," said Martha. "What else could it be?"

"Beats me," said Joe. "And speaking of pictures, don't you think she was hinting there was something else hidden in that picture she gave us?"

"Let's take a look," said Martha, and once again the three Byrams were pouring over the picture.

Even the observant Tad was stumped.

Suddenly, Joe let out a cry. "It can't be!" he said in such a loud voice that the other passengers on the bus turned around and stared.

"What?" cried Tad and Martha in unison.

"Here," said Joe. "Half hidden by the fat lady."

"It looks like—" began Martha.

"But it can't be," interrupted Tad.

"That would be impossible," agreed Joe. "But it might just explain some of the things I was saying about—"

"No," interrupted Tad. "I guess it's just an amazing coincidence."

"Too amazing," said Joe.

Edith, meanwhile, felt as though she were entering another world. For a city, it was overwhelmingly quiet: few cars, no trucks, no motorcycles, just an occasional horsedrawn wagon moving slowly down the cobblestone street. Even the streetlights were different. They look like gas lamps, thought Edith, eyeing the soft, flickering light. They're really pretty, nicer than the ones we have now.

Edith ran as fast as she could down the quiet street. Twice she slipped on the cobblestones and fell. Out of breath, frightened, and with a painful bruise on one elbow, Edith at last careened into a dark alleyway. Leaning against a brick wall, she gasped for breath.

When she'd caught her breath and her heart had stopped thumping quite so loudly, Edith sat down and

44

tried to read the hospital's record book by the glow of the streetlight. But it was too dark to decipher all the tiny, cramped handwriting.

"It'll have to wait till morning," Edith decided, looking around at the bleak alleyway. She considered trying to return to the present for the night but decided against the idea. So she leaned up against the wall and tried to get to sleep.

I never stole anything before, she was thinking. I've hardly ever lied. And I never slept outside before, and all alone, and in the middle of a city. I wonder what Mother would think. I bet Joe, Tad, and Martha never had an adventure like this! I just hope Aunt Margaret won't worry too much.

Still worrying, Edith fell into an uneasy slumber.

Edith rose with the sun and immediately got to work on the hospital's records.

I may not be good at some things, she thought, but I am good at skimming through books for information.

She read page after page. At first it seemed that Rosamond must have been mistaken about which hospital Timothy had been sent to. There was no mention anywhere of a Timothy Byram. But there *was* a record of a Timothy Brian, a four-year-old boy brought to the hospital in September of 1912. And there was another child admitted at the same time, a Brian Thomas. Different people had been responsible for entering information at different times. Some had entered the patient's name in a regular manner: first name first, last name second. Others, however, had been more formal, putting last names first and first names second.

So, thought Edith, first of all, by mistake they called Timothy Byram by the name Timothy Brian. I guess he was too sick to correct them. Then I'll bet they got him confused with Brian Thomas.

And sure enough, a page or two later came the notation that a Timothy Brian had died but a Brian Thomas had recovered. However, being an orphan, he'd been sent to an orphanage in another part of Boston.

Edith jotted down the address and thought rapidly to herself. If he was sent there ten years ago, there's a chance he could still be there. I'll go to the orphanage right away!

But before she headed off, Edith did two things. First she took a photograph of herself back in 1922, using her camera's self-timer. Then she wrote a note saying "Please return to the hospital," put it on top of the roster, and left everything in the doorway of a shop. After a breakfast of cookies from her knapsack, she found her way to the address she'd written down: the orphanage where Brian Thomas had been sent.

"Heavens to Betsy!" exclaimed a cheerful woman when Edith had finished asking her questions. "You're four years too late, child."

"You mean the orphanage isn't here anymore?"

"They closed it four years ago this month. 'Twas when I bought the house; that's why I remember."

"But what happened to the kids who lived here?" cried Edith.

The woman looked kindly at her. She also seemed to be examining Edith's clothing with interest but didn't say anything out loud. "Why don't you step inside, dear," she said. "I'll tell you what I can."

It was a discouraged Edith who sat in a sitting room in 1922 and listened. Even the excitement of being in the past was wearing off. It was becoming all too clear that her mission had been a failure.

I can't do anything right, Edith was thinking as the woman talked.

"So you see, when the woman who ran the orphanage started growing infirm, it was decided that the place should be shut down. Once they'd decided to close it, the authorities either transferred the children to other orphanages or were able to place them in homes."

"I'm looking for one child in particular," said Edith. "There must be some record of where he was sent."

The woman eyed Edith with sympathy, and then shook her head. "There is one thing I do remember," she said. "Shortly before the orphanage was to be shut down, a boy ran away."

"Was he ever found?"

"No," said the woman with certainty. "Brian was his name, I believe, Brian Thomas. Yes, that was it. You see, it was big news around here. All the papers ran the story."

There was no more to be said.

"Thanks," said Edith glumly and wandered off into the streets of Boston.

What's the point of even going back? Edith thought. I'll never be able to find Timothy, never. And that means . . . She hardly liked even thinking about it. But she had to.

That means, thought Edith grimly, we're all going to fade away, just like in the photograph.

Without even looking around her, Edith slipped on the ring and walked through a doorway into a small shop. The owner looked up in shock to see a tall girl vanish before his very eyes.

Edith found herself back in the room that wasn't there. To her great relief, she found Tamburlaine waiting for her, the owl on his shoulder.

"I didn't find him!" she cried. "I'll tell you about it in a minute, but first I'd better go tell Aunt Margaret I'm all right. She must be worried about me."

"Why should she be worried? You haven't been gone that long."

"But . . ."

"Come," said Tamburlaine, ushering Edith through the door into his log cabin. "Come and sit, and I will tell you what I can."

Soon she was relaxing on the sofa by the fireplace. The fox even permitted Edith to hold him in her lap.

"It is but one of the ways that time works," explained Tamburlaine. "Unless you stayed away for months and months, it still would be only at most a few hours in current time."

"That's kind of hard to understand," said Edith.

"Perhaps it is better not to even try."

A few minutes later Tamburlaine shook his head thoughtfully as Edith told him what happened.

"It will take several tries, perhaps, to perfect your aim. You will do better next time."

"Next time!" cried Edith. "We've lost him. He vanished without a trace."

"Not entirely," said Tamburlaine. "He *did* leave a trace: We know his name. It will help us."

"But how? I've failed," cried Edith miserably.

"You did not fail," said Tamburlaine firmly. "You were terribly brave."

"You know," said Edith sheepishly, "that night I spent in the alley, I did think of coming back to Bluebird Hall, just overnight."

"Then *I* would have failed," said Tamburlaine.

"What do you mean?"

"Come," said Tamburlaine, gesturing through an open window toward the field of seven willows behind his cabin. "Let us stroll a bit, and I will tell you more."

The leaves of the willows were rustling in a gentle wind. If this is the same wind of time that blew in the room that wasn't there, thought Edith, here at least, in Tamburlaine's country, it is in a better mood.

Edith saw a pair of swallows darting in the blue sky. She was contentedly watching them when Tamburlaine spoke.

"You cannot go twice to the same place," he said. "You see, when you arrive in the past from the present, you break through the walls of time. It creates a scar, and this scar has to heal properly before you can return to the same place."

"How long does that take?"

"It takes at least ten years of the local time."

"That's too bad," said Edith. "I was just thinking that I could try going back to the hospital a second time. Maybe this time I'd arrive when Timothy was actually there."

"No," said Tamburlaine, "you cannot go to the same place twice."

"It's a good thing I didn't come back that night," said Edith. "Then we wouldn't even know Timothy's new name."

"That is true," said Tamburlaine, pausing near a lively stream to watch the sunlight play in the long, drooping branches of a willow.

For a moment the two watched in silence.

"Edith," said Tamburlaine finally, "now that you know Timothy's name, what will you do?"

"Can't *you* tell me?" asked Edith hopefully.

"I am afraid you must find the way on your own," replied Tamburlaine.

"The library," said Edith. "I'll go to the library. Something will turn up. It has to."

7

INVESTIGATIONS

"Edith," said Mrs. Byram at dinner that night, "you look tired. Have you been working too hard at your writing?"

Edith looked up dreamily. "What did you say, Aunt Margaret?"

"I said, you look as though you've been working too hard."

"No, I haven't even started my writing really," said Edith. "I've . . . been doing other things."

"Well," said Mrs. Byram, "I'm glad you've been enjoying yourself. Just get that writing done. Otherwise, your mother will never let me hear the end of it."

Edith nodded absentmindedly. She was still thinking about Timothy.

"Edith," continued Mrs. Byram, "let me feel your forehead. . . . Just as I thought, a slight fever."

"But I feel—"

"Let's be on the safe side," Mrs. Byram interrupted. "It's to bed with you. I don't want you getting a cold."

"Something is up with Edith," whispered Joe to Tad and Martha as they were cleaning up after dinner. Mrs. Byram was on the phone, and Edith was in her room.

"What do you mean?" asked Tad, his scientific look gleaming in his brown eyes.

"I mean magic," said Joe. "She has that weird sort of glow in her eyes."

"Not Edith," insisted Martha. "It must be her fever. She's just not the kind to find magic. She doesn't even believe in it."

"But she did say that she hadn't started writing," Tad pointed out. "What has she been up to?"

"You didn't show her Great-aunt Ruth's photograph?" Martha asked Joe. "We agreed we'd all do it together, so we could watch her reaction."

"No, I didn't show her the picture," said Joe. "She's got this way all on her own."

"Tomorrow then," said Martha. "We'll show her the photograph tomorrow when she's feeling better. I can't wait!"

While Tad and Martha finished washing up, Mrs. Byram sent Joe upstairs with a cup of tea for Edith. Joe found his cousin sitting on her bed, staring at the door that led nowhere. She looked as though she had something important on her mind.

Joe looked hard at Edith. Why was she so nervous?

"Edith," he began, but then paused. He didn't know quite what to say. "Edith," repeated Joe.

"Yes?"

"Um, here's some tea. I hope you'll feel better tomorrow."

"I'm sure I will," said Edith. "At least I hope so."

Edith spent the morning in the library but had no luck. She looked through every reference book she could think of, including phone books for all of New England, trying to find some reference to Brian Thomas.

At lunch, Mrs. Byram noticed that Edith looked a bit down. "What's the matter, dear?" she asked. "Isn't your writing going well?"

"No," sighed Edith. "I needed to find some information, and I just couldn't."

"Well, I wouldn't worry. You're such a bright girl, I know you'll find it. And even if you can't, I'm sure it's not *that* important."

"That's what you think," said Edith.

"Edith," said Mrs. Byram, "can I give you a bit of advice? School *is* very important, but you're only twelve. You don't have to worry about it quite so much."

"It's not schoolwork I'm worrying about," began Edith. "It's . . ." Then she stopped. Somehow, she didn't think her aunt would understand.

"Is it your mother?" asked Mrs. Byram gently. "Well," she said, "perhaps she and I will have a little talk."

The backdoor swinging open interrupted them. Turning around, they discovered Great-aunt Ruth.

"I'm in the middle of doing errands," she announced. "Let's see, what was it I had to do over here?"

"Sit down, dear," said Mrs. Byram. "I'm sure it will come to you. Edith and I were just chatting."

"Hello, Edith," said Great-aunt Ruth with a smile. "I

know!" she cried suddenly. "Have you seen today's paper?"

Soon Ruth had opened it to a certain page, and Mrs. Byram was reading a certain article and laughing derisively.

"What's so amusing?" asked Edith.

"Look at this photograph!" chuckled Mrs. Byram.

"Oh, my word," said Ruth. "I can hardly stand the sight of him!"

"Of who?" asked Edith.

"It's an article about Horatio Snivell," explained Mrs. Byram, showing Edith a photograph of a small man with a pinched-up face. "He's just been made highway commissioner."

"He's not much to look at," agreed Edith, "but why do you dislike him so much?"

"The Byrams and the Snivells have never gotten along," said Mrs. Byram. "Those Snivells are always try-ing to get their greedy hands on Bluebird Hall."

"It almost happened again just last fall," added Ruth. "Mercifully, it didn't come to pass. You know," she con-tinued, "it would break my heart to think of Bluebird Hall in anyone else's hands—the house, the land, and the old family graveyard out back. My father is there; yours, too," she told Edith. "Only Byrams have been laid to rest there, never anyone else."

"Ruth," said Mrs. Byram, changing the topic, "surely you didn't drive all the way over to show us a photograph of Horatio Snivell?"

"Of course not. I wanted to drop off a new print of the

picture of Tad, Martha, and Joe. You know, the one that was fading."

"Why, thank you, Ruth. That's very kind of you. I don't know why they all got so upset about that picture. It's not like them."

"It is a *bit* troubling," said Ruth mysteriously. "Anyway, let's hope this photo stays as it is."

"Well," said Mrs. Byram, "now that that's done, can I offer you some tea?"

"Thank you, no. I'm on my way to drop off a painting of mine at Simon Andrews's house."

"Simon who?" asked Edith.

"Simon Andrews," said Great-aunt Ruth, "the painter."

"I didn't know he was still painting," said Mrs. Byram.

"He's not," said Ruth. "He's been too ill for a long time."

"Such a pity," commented Mrs. Byram.

"I know," said Ruth. "You see, Edith, I've admired his work for ever so long. Then, finally, I wrote him a letter in care of his gallery. Imagine my surprise when I discovered he'd been living only about twenty miles from here for the past ten years or so, down the road in Woodbury."

"It's funny you never ran into him," observed Edith.

"It seems he is a bit of a recluse," said Ruth. "But he did write back. We even spoke on the phone and were making plans to meet when he took seriously ill. I understand he's entirely bedridden and sees no one—except his house-keeper, of course. So we never got to meet. But once in a while I drop off something at his house—grapes or a loaf of bread. Today I'm dropping off a small painting of mine. I do hope he'll like it."

"I'm sure he will, Ruth," said Mrs. Byram.

"By the way, Edith," said Ruth, getting up to go, "how did you like the photograph I gave Tad, Martha, and Joe?"

"You mean the one of them?" asked Edith.

"Goodness no, I mean the other one."

"I'm afraid we haven't seen it yet," said Mrs. Byram. "Come to think of it, I did pass Martha's room and saw them all huddled together, examining something."

"Well, do take a look at it," said Great-aunt Ruth, speaking to both Mrs. Byram and Edith, but looking especially hard at Edith, as though she were trying to make sense of something she couldn't quite remember.

8

GREENVALE, 1923

Tamburlaine smiled happily. Even the owl perched on his shoulder appeared pleased.

"Look," Edith said. "The poster even says the exact date and place: Greenvale, April eighteenth, nineteen twenty-three."

Lunch was over and Edith had made her way to the room that wasn't there. Once again she was in luck. Tamburlaine's door was there, waiting for her.

Soon she and Tamburlaine were seated on the sofa, looking at the circus photograph that Great-aunt Ruth had given Tad, Martha, and Joe. Edith had borrowed it from Martha's room.

Edith had seen the name Brian Thomas on the circus poster the second she picked up the photograph on Martha's desk. She had gone at once to show Tamburlaine.

After he'd examined the photograph with care, Tamburlaine said, "I also see something else. This, I believe, is what made your cousins so excited. Remember, only *you* know Timothy's assumed name."

With Tamburlaine watching, Edith looked hard at the picture. Then she gave a cry of astonishment. "It can't be!" she said. "How . . ."

"How did *you* get in that picture?" asked Tamburlaine, finishing the sentence for her.

"I guess," said Edith, "it must mean this is the right Brian Thomas."

Tamburlaine smiled.

"Tamburlaine," said Edith, "I never told you, but when I went back in time to Boston, there was one second when I looked down. And . . ."

"What did you see?"

"For a second I saw this place. It looked like a bog, with heavy mist everywhere. It was filled with people, and they all were lost, crying for help. Then it was gone. I thought maybe I was just seeing things that weren't there."

Tamburlaine bowed his head. "No," he said gently, "what you saw was there."

"Is that what would happen if . . . I mean, unless I can get my grandfather?"

"It will not happen," Tamburlaine said. "It *must* not." He handed Edith a large package. "I have a surprise for you."

"For me?" said Edith.

"It is from Rosamond. She managed to leave it for you in the room. She was very brave to try entering it again."

In the package was a velvet dress with a lace collar, matching hair ribbons, a small brooch, and a pair of brown leather boots.

Edith could tell everything would fit perfectly.

Excusing herself, she darted into an adjoining room in Tamburlaine's cabin and put on the clothes. The old-fashioned look suited her. She used the ribbons to do up her hair the way she'd seen Rosamond wear hers.

"I look really pretty," said Edith in amazement.

"Of course you do," said Tamburlaine. "You always have."

There was a note at the bottom of the package. Edith read it out loud.

"Dear Edith," she read, "I cannot thank you enough for looking for Timothy. I really miss him. Perhaps you can understand that. Thank you again. Rosamond."

Edith laid the note down gently.

"I *can* understand," she said. "I still miss my dad, and it's been years."

"I know," said Tamburlaine.

Soon it was time to go.

"I'll do better this time," said Edith. "After all, Greenvale isn't that far from Rock Ridge."

"And now you will fit right in," added Tamburlaine.

"Tamburlaine," said Edith, "do you think that Timothy will like me?"

"Of course he will," replied Tamburlaine. "But I'd suggest that you tell him about himself gradually. Coming out of the blue, it might be a terrible shock."

"I just wish I weren't going all by myself," said Edith.

"Perhaps you are not."

"Tamburlaine!" cried Edith. "Are you coming with me?"

"No, not I," said Tamburlaine, "although you will

never be far from me, in my thoughts. But *she* is."

Tamburlaine's white owl, looking like the glow of the moon on a misty night, flapped her wings and glided from Tamburlaine's shoulder to Edith's.

"You will be joining a circus," explained Tamburlaine. "A performing owl might come in handy."

"Is she trained?" asked Edith.

Tamburlaine smiled a faraway smile. "Sometimes," he said, "I think that she trained me. No, she is not trained in the regular sense of the word; but what you tell her to do, she will do. Within reason, of course. Owls are proud creatures."

"Does she have to carry her own ring?"

"No," said Tamburlaine, "but when you voyage out and when you return, she must be touching you. That is enough. Now, it is time." Tamburlaine bowed his head in thought. "Much depends on finding Timothy. Many lives, and much happiness, hang in the balance."

"I can't even get around to writing that story," mumbled Edith. "I don't know how I'll ever be able to find Timothy."

Without another word, Tamburlaine ushered Edith back into the room that wasn't there.

When she entered, Edith felt the wind that whistled through the narrow room die down to a whisper. In her mind's eye, Edith pictured 1923 and the name Greenvale.

Then she opened her eyes.

A door was there on the far wall, strangely bright in the dark room, like the North Star on a black night.

With the owl on her shoulder, Edith approached the

bright door. But at the door she stopped. "No," she said, "I'm not going. Not alone. It's time I told my cousins. Is that all right, Tamburlaine?"

"Whatever you wish cannot be wrong," he said.

"I've just been wanting to go by myself to show off, so I could boast about it later," said Edith.

"As you wish," said Tamburlaine.

With the owl still perched on her shoulder and the ring still on her finger, Edith took a step away from the door. But in her haste, she forgot she was wearing the long skirt that Rosamond had left for her. Somehow she got tangled in the unfamiliar garment and lost her balance.

With a cry, Edith pitched over—right into the door. It flew open. Edith tumbled through and was gone.

Once again there was the sensation of moving rapidly yet standing still, of immense light and bleak darkness just beyond, and of landing hard on the ground without ever really having left it.

Edith looked around. She had landed on the shore of a small pond. Lovely green hills could be seen not too far off. Edith guessed it must be very early in the morning. Birds were singing from a nearby pine forest, and the owl on her shoulder seemed to be listening to them with great interest.

Leaving the pond behind, Edith started walking through the pines. Finally, she came upon a narrow road.

As she followed the road, she met no one. Most of the houses were entirely still.

VILLAGE OF GREENVALE read a sign, and soon Edith and the owl had entered a charming village. Edith had been to Greenvale many times in the present, visiting her Great-aunt Ruth, and Greenvale in the past was remarkably similar.

Peering through a shop window, Edith found it was five thirty in the morning.

A brightly colored poster in front of another shop caught Edith's eye: TWO DAYS ONLY! SHEEHAN'S TRAVELING CIRCUS—FUN FOR YOUNG AND OLD! GREENVALE, APRIL 18TH AND 19TH.

"Right time, right place!" Edith said. "I think I'm really getting the hang of this."

Even the owl looked pleased.

"Yes, my dear," said an old woman in a shawl. "The circus is this very night."

At first Edith had mistaken the old woman for her great-aunt, but then she'd remembered that, back in 1923, Ruth was only thirteen.

"Where exactly will it be?"

"Just beyond town. You're sure to see the fairgrounds."

"Thank you," said Edith aloud, as she thought, Maybe they're already there, setting up.

Soon Edith had reached the fairgrounds. Two young men were hanging a big sign between posts. SHEEHAN'S TRAVELING CIRCUS it boasted in gold letters on an emerald green background. ADMITTANCE: 5¢.

Around the edges of a broad field were brightly painted caravans. Some were for people to live in; others were cages on wheels for transporting animals. Edith saw a few bears, some monkeys, and a sleepy looking tiger. The owl on her shoulder seemed to be examining everything with great interest, too.

A small corral had been erected, and the horses used to pull the caravans were grazing in the lush grass. Some were plain workhorses, while others were evidently part of the show. A pure white one with a flowing mane was especially beautiful. And there was a striking golden-colored horse with a white mane and tail.

A large tent was being raised in the center of the field. Men were already sweating with effort as they pulled on thick ropes and the tent began to take shape.

Surrounding the large tent were a number of smaller tents being decorated with ribbons and signs that read: FORTUNA, THE FORTUNE-TELLER and BERTHA, THE BEARDED LADY — 3¢. Boys were rapidly nailing together a small shed that would be the ticket seller's booth.

"Get 'er nice and tight," instructed a man as an older boy was hammering on a ladder above him.

It was Timothy. There was no doubt about it, he looked so much like Rosamond with blazing blue eyes, a mischievous expression, and tousled hair.

"And he's my grandfather!" Edith marveled.

Soon the job was finished and Edith was able to talk to him. "Are you with the circus?" she asked.

Clear blue eyes looked straight at her. "Yes, I am. I'm Brian Thomas. Who are you?"

"I'm Edith. I'm . . ."

"Yes?"

"I'm . . . I'm looking for work. My owl and I are an act. Do you think there might be a job for us with the circus?"

"Well," said Timothy, "there's just one way to find out. We'll go ask old man Sheehan. Come on.

"So," he said as they walked, "where are you from?"

"Well, you see, to tell the truth, I was in an orphanage in Boston, but I decided to head out on my own."

Timothy looked at Edith. "So you're an orphan, too. So am I. I was really sick and almost died. When I came to, I could hardly remember a thing. The nurse kept saying, 'Brian, Brian, you've pulled through.' I didn't even recognize my own name! I learned that my parents, my brother, and I had all been sick, and only I survived. I could barely feel sad, though, since I couldn't remember them. So I wound up in an orphanage. But when I ran away, I picked a new name: Timothy. Most everyone calls me that."

"It's a good name," said Edith.

Suddenly Timothy stopped. "Not too many girls would run away alone to join a circus. Or boys, either."

"Well," Edith said, "I do have my owl."

"You know," said Timothy, "you remind me of someone." He shook his head.

"What are you thinking about?" asked Edith.

"Sometimes I almost remember something. I remember a big white house near a broad field. And someone who looks like me. But I don't think it is the brother the nurse mentioned. It is someone else. Anyway, here we are—old man Sheehan's caravan. Let's hope your act impresses the boss!"

WHITE WONDER

"Don't usually hire girls," muttered a gruff, middle-aged man, "and I've never heard of a trained owl. But if you're any good, you've got a job."

Wishing she'd practiced a bit, Edith stepped forward uncertainly.

"Ladies and gentlemen, boys and girls," Edith began, trying to act the way Martha would. "I hereby present the world's wisest owl. Her name is . . ." Edith hesitated for a moment, but then she remembered the name on the poster. ". . . the world's wisest owl," Edith continued. "Her name is the White Wonder. Your wish is her command."

"Now let's see what the bird can do," said Mr. Sheehan.

"White Wonder," Edith asked the owl, "what is two plus two?"

The owl hooted four times.

"Good," said Mr. Sheehan.

"White Wonder," commanded Edith, "bring me the handkerchief from the man's coat pocket."

Making a swift loop through the morning air, the owl sailed past Mr. Sheehan's chest. In a flash, she grabbed the handkerchief and brought it back to Edith, depositing it in the girl's open hand before resuming her perch on Edith's shoulder.

"Very good," said Mr. Sheehan appreciatively.

"That's the ticket," said Timothy.

"White Wonder," commanded Edith, "return the handkerchief to the gentleman, but place it in his right pocket this time."

"Mighty smart," said Mr. Sheehan when the handkerchief had been returned to his right pocket. "However did you train her? Owls are such ornery birds."

"I think she trained me," said Edith, remembering Tamburlaine's words.

"So," asked Timothy, "does she have the job?"

"She sure does," said Mr. Sheehan, shaking Edith's hand. "Welcome to Sheehan's Traveling Circus!"

The next few hours passed very quickly. Timothy had to go off and set up for that night's performance, and Edith had to have a circus costume altered to fit her. Once that was done, she strolled around. There was a lot to see, and the circus folk seemed very friendly.

"So you're a friend of Timothy's?" asked an enormous woman, sitting on a crate and eating some brown bread.

"Yes, I'm Edith."

"Sit down, my dear, and have a chat," said the woman, giving the owl a piece of bread, which it gobbled hungrily. "I'm Bertha, the Bearded Lady."

"But . . ." began Edith.

"But where's my beard?" said Bertha, giving a chuckle. "That old beard itches something brutal. Young lady," Bertha said in a different tone, "I hope you're not planning to join the circus."

"I already did," said Edith happily.

Bertha looked around nervously, then said in a low voice, "Sheehan's Traveling Circus is no place for a girl. It's haunted. The ghost of poor George put a curse on it, I swear he has."

"What do you mean?" asked Edith.

"George Dickinson used to work with Sheehan's Circus. There was an accident one night," Bertha explained. "George was dismantling the main tent and he fell. And ever since then he's haunted us. We've left behind four men so far."

"What do you mean left behind?"

"I mean in a grave," said Bertha sadly. "You see, the men who hire on to help with the heavy work have no real home. So Seamus—Mr. Sheehan—pays for their burial. And each time, right before one of the men has died, we've heard George's ghost moaning. Sad to say, some say they heard the ghost last night."

The owl seemed to shake her wise head in disbelief, while Edith was shaking hers in wonder.

Edith and Timothy sat on a stone wall, sharing a lunch of bread and cheese. It was a warm April afternoon now that the wind had died down.

"Why do you keep looking at me?" asked Timothy.

"I guess you remind me of someone I know," said Edith.

And that really was true. Joe did bear an amazing resemblance to his grandfather.

"That's odd," said Timothy, "because you remind me of someone."

"Actually," began Edith when shouts echoed from one of the caravans.

A man was crying out in an anguished voice and people were quickly gathering. Edith and Timothy joined them.

Inside the brightly painted caravan lay one of the hired hands. "It's my chest," he gasped. "I can barely move, it hurts so much."

Another of the men bowed his head solemnly. "May the ghost we heard last night not have been wailing for him."

"Back to work, back to work," said a gruff voice behind them.

"But Mr. Sheehan," someone said, "it's Mike. He's not well."

"Then I'll send Bridget to look after him," barked Mr. Sheehan.

"Bridget's his wife," Timothy whispered to Edith. "Anyway, I've got to get back to work myself or I'll be in trouble. I'm afraid you're on your own for a while."

"I've got to work on my act," said Edith. "Then, after the show, there's something I want to talk about. Something important."

"Yes?" said Timothy, his eyes alight with curiosity.

But just then Edith's eyes widened and her mouth fell open. "What's *he* doing here?" she gasped.

"What are you talking about?"

"That man just behind you," said Edith. "The small one with the sour expression. How'd he get here?"

"It isn't *that* far from Rock Ridge to Greenvale," Timothy said, laughing. "You can even walk it, if you have the time."

"You mean you know him?"

"'Fraid so." Timothy sighed. "Horatio Snivell is some kind of bigwig over in Rock Ridge. He's always snooping around, making sure we follow all the little rules he makes up. He even fined Mr. Sheehan for not having his license properly posted! But why do you ask?"

"'Cause he *really* looks like someone I know," explained Edith.

"Maybe they're related," said Timothy.

"They are," said Edith, half to herself.

"Now," said Timothy, "what was it we were talking about?"

"About getting back to work," boomed a voice behind them.

"Yes, Mr. Sheehan," said Timothy. "I'll be right there."

Edith noticed a gentle-looking woman leaving the caravan where the sick man was lying.

"Is he all right?" she asked the woman.

"Mike?" said the woman. "Well, I did soothe him a bit with some tonic, but I don't like the way he looks. Just pray the ghost wasn't wailing for him, poor soul."

"Is that story really true?"

"Who can doubt it?" asked the woman. "Four times someone has heard the ghost wail; four times men have died. We heard it in Lenox, we heard it in Greenfield, we heard it in Great Barrington, and we heard it in Northampton. And now we've heard it here in Greenvale."

After Mrs. Sheehan left her, Edith watched the circus folk getting ready for that night's show, often singing to themselves as they did. Bertha was combing out her beard, preparing to attach it, while the animal trainer was busy grooming his animals. Others were polishing woodwork or counting money or preparing food to sell. The owl seemed to be observing the circus folk as carefully as Edith.

Yet there was an air of unease. The ghost was on almost everyone's mind.

"Did you find the circus, girl?"

Edith wheeled around. After she finished rehearsing her act, she'd taken a stroll into Greenvale and was so enjoying the beauty of the town back in 1923 that she hadn't even seen the old woman approaching her.

"You're the one who gave me directions this morning, aren't you?" said Edith. "Thank you. I found it with no trouble. Will you be there tonight?"

The old woman smiled. "We don't get too much entertainment passing through Greenvale, so you can bet just about everyone will be over at Sheehan's Circus tonight. 'Twas a hard winter, you know. In fact, it's a hard old world, and getting harder all the time. Why, the robbers these days will take anything that's not nailed down."

"Well," said Edith, "if you think crime's bad now, you should see what it's like where I come from."

"It couldn't be worse than it is now," said the woman. "There has been a string of robberies all around this part of Massachusetts. Lennox. Greenfield. Northampton. Great Barrington. Silver and jewels stolen, and then they simply vanish! The robbers must be hiding it somewhere, but no one knows where. But enough, I must be off. I'll be looking for you at the circus."

"See you then!" called Edith.

It happened at the same moment Edith was chatting with the old woman, only it was three-quarters of a century later.

Actually, quite a few things happened.

First, Martha noticed that the photograph of the circus was missing. She was sure she'd left it on her desk.

"Mom," she called, "did you take anything from my room?"

"Of course not, dear," came the reply.

"Tad, Joe," said Martha in a loud voice, "come quick!"

Her brothers appeared in Martha's room at the same time, and each had a worried look on his face.

"The picture's gone," said Martha, "and Mom didn't take it. Did either of you?"

Tad and Joe shook their heads.

"Then it had to be Edith. I think we should go ask her."

"That's just it," burst out Joe. "We can't."

"What do you mean we can't?"

"I mean," said Joe, "that Edith has vanished. I've looked everywhere. And I mean everywhere."

"Oh, she's probably just at the library," said Martha.

"It's six o'clock," said Joe. "The library's closed."

"Then she's out taking a walk," interrupted Tad. "And who cares? There's something we have to talk about." And with that he shut the door so their mother couldn't overhear and took out the photograph that Great-aunt Ruth had dropped off that afternoon. He laid it on Martha's desk.

Joe and Martha stepped closer to get a good look.

"Look," said Tad in a low voice. "We're half gone already."

"But that's impossible," cried Martha. "I mean, even if Great-aunt Ruth made a mistake once, she wouldn't make it twice."

"No," said Joe. "It's not a mistake. It's magic."

"Magic!" Martha whistled. "We've been looking for it, but instead it's found us!"

"Good grief, Martha," said Tad. "Something terrible is going to happen. It probably is happening already. I can feel it."

"I feel it, too," said Joe. "I think we should take another look at the photo of the circus that Great-aunt Ruth gave us. I'm sure she was trying to tell us something. And I bet it involves Edith somehow."

"Not Edith!" said Martha.

"Joe's right," said Tad. "The girl in the circus picture *did* look like Edith."

"But how would Edith get in a picture taken in 1923?" demanded Martha.

Her brothers cast her a long look.

"Maybe the same way we did," said Tad. "If *we* could find magic, why couldn't Edith?"

"Maybe magic runs in the Byram family," Joe said.

"Great-aunt Ruth has found it. And now Edith has, too."

Once Martha was convinced, they sprang into action.

Martha tried to reach Great-aunt Ruth on the phone. Tad searched Bluebird Hall's extensive grounds, just in case Edith was out taking a walk. Joe kept watch on Edith's room. None of them had any luck. Great-aunt Ruth was out, and neither Tad nor Joe found any trace of Edith anywhere.

Martha ended up sitting by the phone, trying Ruth's number every few minutes; Tad sat on the stone wall behind the house, thinking; and Joe stationed himself in the upstairs hallway.

But Edith didn't appear.

She might have been only a few miles distant, but she was very far away.

Timothy was so excited, Edith could hardly get a word in edgewise. He was going to ride one of the horses that night! He and Edith would both be in the big ring. Their names were even put on the poster by the ticket seller's booth.

And it was a wonderful circus, thought Edith as she watched from behind a screen. The trained bears, the tiger, the acrobats, the clowns—each received deafening applause.

And Timothy was excellent. Dressed in chaps and a tall hat, and called "Brian Thomas, the Colorado Cowboy," he rode a palomino bareback.

Edith cheered everyone, but she cheered Timothy the most.

After intermission, it was Edith's turn to go on.

She stood frozen when she heard Mr. Sheehan announcing her act through a megaphone: "The lovely Edith and the White Wonder!"

Timothy had to give her a friendly shove into the spotlight.

A sprinkling of polite applause welcomed her, but the owl's first trick got everyone's attention.

By the time Edith told the owl to fly into the audience and come back with something red, and the owl did, the crowd was shouting for more.

Timothy was cheering as Edith and the owl left the sawdust ring.

Too soon the evening was over, and a happy crowd was slowly making its way home.

But when Edith and Timothy went behind the main tent to find some water for the owl, the mood there was strangely somber.

"It's Mike," said Hugh, one of the hired hands. "He passed on during the show."

"So," said Mark, another handyman, "the ghost *was* wailing for him."

"Oh, there's no such thing as ghosts," said another man.

"Ghost or no ghost," said Hugh, "Mrs. Sheehan says we'll be burying him tomorrow morning, first thing."

Edith was too shaken by the news to talk any further with Timothy.

"I'll do it tomorrow," she said. "Tomorrow is time enough."

10

BLUEBIRD HALL, 1923

"Let us pray," intoned the priest as Mike's coffin was lowered into the ground.

It was a foggy, drizzly morning, and most of the circus folk were gathered around an open grave in a small cemetery located on a quiet hillside. Edith could hardly believe where they were.

A while earlier, everyone had gathered outside Mr. Sheehan's caravan, then had loaded themselves into wagons to go to the cemetery.

"Where are we going?" asked Edith as the wagon rattled along.

"Rock Ridge," said Timothy. "A family there has a private graveyard."

"What's the family name?" asked Edith excitedly.

"Byram," answered someone else. "They live in a big house called Bluebird Hall."

"Bluebird Hall!" gasped Edith. Her head was spinning. What if Rosamond is home from school? she thought. Would she have met me yet?

Even Edith couldn't unravel these riddles, so she sat back to see how Rock Ridge looked back in 1923.

Large empty meadows looked lovely even in the drizzle. Edith knew that in the present these same meadows had become shopping malls or housing developments.

"It really was a lot prettier back then," she said.

"Back when?" Timothy asked as they neared Bluebird Hall.

"I'll tell you later."

"Edith," said Timothy, "you are a most mysterious girl."

He, too, seemed to be examining the scenery with care. "It's strange," he said to Edith, "but this town looks familiar to me, too."

Down Bluebird Hall's long drive they rolled.

The large white house looked the same. Its comfortable elegance almost seemed to welcome Edith back.

They stopped in front of the house, and Mr. Sheehan knocked on the door.

A girl opened it, but no one Edith recognized, at least not at first. It certainly wasn't Rosamond, though the girl had the same penetrating blue eyes.

Then Edith knew: the eyes, the expression, the somewhat stocky figure. Of course, her hair wasn't gray and her face was unwrinkled, but it was Great-aunt Ruth!

"I'm Ruth Byram," said the girl to Mr. Sheehan. "Father's taken Mother to Albany this morning. She's been ill, I'm afraid. I'll be joining them later. But I've been expecting you. I'll show you the way to our graveyard."

So there they stood, watching the coffin being lowered.

Heads were bowed in sadness and respect. To Edith's surprise, Mr. Snivell showed up. He brought his wife,

Mabel, whose face was as pinched and ratlike as his own. He acted as though he were in charge of the entire proceedings.

Once when he wasn't looking, Edith saw Ruth stick out her tongue at him.

The only person crying was Mrs. Sheehan.

"She's so softhearted, she cries when it rains," Timothy whispered to Edith.

Mrs. Sheehan was sobbing as the crowd left the cemetery.

"Now, now, don't carry on so," said Bertha.

"I went to check on him during the show," said Mrs. Sheehan, "just to bring him a cup of tea. But it was too late even to fetch the doctor. So I just called Mark and Hugh."

"Mark and Hugh are two other handymen," Timothy explained. "They've built coffins for the other four men who died."

Ruth had kindly invited them all back to the house for hot coffee after the burial.

How wonderful it was to be in Bluebird Hall. Somehow it was starting to feel more like Edith's home than the apartment back in New York City.

Edith volunteered to help Ruth, and soon the two were chatting in the kitchen as they readied coffee and cookies.

Ruth was a spirited thirteen year old who wanted to know everything about circus life.

"I only joined a short time ago," said Edith, "but so far it's been terribly exciting—except for poor Mike, of course."

"I'm thinking of running away to join the circus

myself," Ruth confided a while later, after Edith had explained her act with the owl.

"But why?" gasped Edith. "You've always loved Blue-bird Hall."

"How would you know?" asked Ruth, looking suspiciously at Edith.

"Just a guess," said Edith. "I'm a good guesser."

"Actually, you are," said Ruth, still examining Edith. "And you look oddly familiar. So does that boy you came with. Anyway, I *have* always loved it here. But not lately."

"Why not?"

A sad expression filled Ruth's beautiful eyes.

"Nothing's been right since Timothy died," she said. "He was my brother," she added. "He became ill and was taken to a hospital in Boston. He never came back."

"I'm sorry," said Edith, aching to tell Ruth the truth. But would she believe her? And was she supposed to tell anyone besides Timothy?

"Anyway," continued Ruth, "since then, Mother's gotten ill, and she and Father sent Rosamond off to boarding school. They thought the change of scene might do her good. Rosamond is my older sister. She was Timothy's twin. So, you can see why I want to run away."

"Being in a circus isn't really that great," said Edith. "I bet you'd be a lot happier here."

"If there *is* a here," said Ruth.

"What do you mean?" asked Edith.

"Mother and Father seem to feel that Bluebird Hall is too full of sad memories. There was even some talk of selling it; but I think Father wasn't completely sure because he set a ridiculously high figure, even for the nicest house in Rock Ridge. But that horrible Mr. Snivell said if he could raise the money, he'd pay. Those Snivells have always wanted to get their nasty hands on Bluebird Hall."

"What did your parents say?"

Ruth looked incensed. "They said all right. Mother said it was now in the hands of Fate. If Mr. Snivell could raise the money, that would mean we were supposed to move. If he couldn't, that would mean we're supposed to stay."

"How long did they give him?"

"Until the end of the month."

"But that's ten days away!" cried Edith.

"You seem as upset as I am," said Ruth as the two headed for the living room.

"Well, I just took an instantaneous dislike to Mr. Snivell," said Edith, "and I hate the idea of him living here."

"So do I," said Ruth. "But what can I do? It's not up to me. You can see why I want to join the circus."

"Where is everyone?" asked Edith when she and Ruth returned to the living room.

"Mr. Sheehan remembered a job that needed doing straightaway," explained Mrs. Sheehan, "so, off he went to do it, taking a few of the men with him."

"Where's Timothy?" asked Edith, looking around. "I want him to meet someone."

"I'm sorry, dear," said Mrs. Sheehan, "but he went off with Mr. Sheehan. He told me to tell you that he'd see you back at the circus."

"Where's the coffee?" asked an unpleasant voice.

It was Mr. Snivell, rubbing his small hands together in happy expectation of free food.

Ruth passed the coffee and Edith the cookies.

"Such a tragedy," she overheard Mrs. Sheehan telling Fortuna.

"I foresaw it," the fortune-teller claimed, munching on her cookie.

"More cookies, please," cried Cassia, the circus's fat lady. "I haven't had nearly enough."

"I love the circus folk," whispered Ruth to Edith as they passed.

It was just an hour to opening time. Edith had fed the owl, who'd spent the day dozing, and found Timothy busy at work. Mr. Sheehan had had them build a new stand for Cassia. She was getting too hefty for her old one.

"You two," barked Mr. Sheehan to Timothy and Edith. "I need some extra change. Can the two of you run into town and pick up as much as the shopkeepers can spare?"

Saying this, he handed Timothy a roll of bills.

"He certainly is trusting," said Edith as they started off.

"Maybe too trusting," said Timothy, "considering the way he just hires on all those men without knowing the first thing about them. He tells Mrs. Sheehan to hire anyone who needs work, no questions asked. I can't help but wonder about Mark and Hugh and some of their friends," he added, smoothing down his hair just the way Joe did.

Edith couldn't help but smile. He really did remind her of Joe.

"What's so amusing?" asked Timothy as they entered Greenvale.

80

Edith suddenly became serious. "It has to do with what I want to talk with you about."

"All right, mysterious one, talk."

"It's hard to explain," began Edith when Timothy interrupted.

"Look over there," he said. "That woman. Something must be wrong."

On a corner, near the bakery, Edith saw the old woman she'd spoken with the day before. She was crying.

"Maybe she was a friend of Mike's?" guessed Timothy, as Edith stopped to speak with the old lady.

"No," Edith said to Timothy soon after. "She is crying because she's been robbed. All of her beautiful old silver was stolen while she was at the circus."

The color disappeared from Timothy's face. "That is a very strange coincidence," he said. "You see, every time one of the men has died, there's been a robbery that night. They've never caught the robbers, and what's more, the stolen goods have just disappeared."

"Hmmm," said Edith, thinking out loud, "robberies the nights the men have died. Were they in the same town where the circus was?"

Timothy thought a moment. "If not the exact same town, then one nearby," he said.

"So most people would be at the circus. The town would be nearly empty. What a perfect time for a robbery!"

"You're right," said Timothy. "But tell me this, where are they hiding the loot? And *why* are they hiding it?"

"They're hiding it until the furor dies down, then they can retrieve it."

•

"From where?" said Timothy, puzzled.

"I think I know," said Edith. "In the coffins. It's the perfect hiding place. Later, they'll come back and dig it up."

"Digging up a corpse just to get some silver? Nobody would do something so disgusting."

"Who says there's a corpse?" asked Edith. "I think those men never died at all. They just sneaked off into the night. Probably they were paid to leave quietly."

"But who would do that?" asked Timothy.

"The person planning it all, that's who. It might be the person who supposedly found all the men dead."

"Not Mrs. Sheehan," said Timothy. "She's so nice!"

"It has to be somebody," said Edith. She couldn't tell Timothy, but Edith had just remembered something: No one but a Byram was ever buried in the family graveyard at Bluebird Hall.

"How do you know so much?" asked Timothy.

"I'll tell you later," said Edith hurriedly. "There's only one thing to do now. How brave are you?"

"As brave as you, I guess," said Timothy. "Why?"

"Tonight," vowed Edith, "we're going to find out just what's in Mike's grave."

11

IN AN OPEN GRAVE

The church clock in the village was striking midnight when Edith and Timothy met just outside the main circus tent. Each was armed with a shovel, borrowed from the circus's equipment caravan, and they both had a look of grim determination on their faces.

"Maybe we shouldn't be doing this," whispered Edith, "but . . ."

"But we have to," finished Timothy. "If we can do something to stop the thieves, then we should."

"Maybe we could just tell the police," suggested Edith.

"No, they would never believe us." Timothy harnessed one of the workhorses to a cart. "The police don't trust circus folk."

The horse and cart rolled through the sleeping village of Greenvale.

ROCK RIDGE, 3 MILES read a sign. Timothy had asked Edith to drive the horse and cart. To her great surprise, she turned out to be good at it.

As they neared Rock Ridge, Timothy was wondering aloud exactly what they'd find in Mike's grave.

Edith had something different on her mind. The night was dark and still, and it seemed a good time to talk. She looked over at Timothy. It would take a lot of believing on his part to accept that he was really her grandfather when he was only fifteen years old! Maybe I should wait until this is all over, thought Edith, but she had to ask herself if she was stalling because she was enjoying this adventure with Timothy. Just then they arrived at the narrow dirt road leading to the graveyard. At Timothy's suggestion, they hid the horse and cart and finished the journey on foot.

Soon they arrived at the small Byram graveyard. A large yew tree blocked the little shaft of moonlight that shone through the massing rain clouds.

In the present, thought Edith, both her father and her cousins' father were buried here. She was glad she was in the past.

Mike's grave was easy to find. The large rectangle of soil was loose and bare. No tombstone had been erected, just a wooden cross with Mike's name.

"After you," said Edith grimly.

Into the dark soil slipped Timothy's shovel, and soon a load of dirt went flying onto the grass bordering the grave.

It was a chilly night, yet soon sweat was pouring off them. Thunder boomed in the distance and a bat darted by, but Timothy and Edith kept digging. Two feet down, they paused to rest, sitting on the side of the grave just as a fine mist started.

"If it really is Mike in there," said Timothy, "then what we're doing is terrible. And probably illegal, too."

"He's not in there," said Edith. "He can't be."

Once again dirt flew. By this time rain was falling, and the gravestones seemed to glow with moisture. They were a pale silver, and it almost appeared that they were watching. Nearly every one had the name "Byram" engraved on it.

"I keep getting this creepy feeling," Edith whispered.

An hour later they had dug down so far that Edith's head was right below ground level. Timothy, who was taller, could still see out. They were too out of breath to even speak. Digging took all their energy.

A dog howled in the distance, guarding a house somewhere. The rain was steady now, chilling Edith and Timothy to the bone.

With a loud clang, the church clock in Rock Ridge struck two in the morning, disturbing some crows huddled in the yew tree. With a sudden rush of wings and some hoarse cries, the birds took flight, swooping over the open grave like a dark cloud.

"It's like a bad dream," said Edith, shivering.

Still they dug, deeper and deeper.

The dark of night and the falling rain seemed to be closing in on them when Timothy gave a sudden cry. "I think I hit something."

He fell to his knees and poked around in the soggy earth where his shovel had struck wood.

Edith gasped. "We're standing on the coffin!"

"What did you think we were standing on?" asked

Timothy, using his shovel to clear off the top of the pine box.

Soon the lid of the coffin had been uncovered and they had hollowed out an area to one side where they could kneel as they finished the job.

"I can't look," Edith said. "What if it's Mike? I think I'd faint."

"You won't faint," said Timothy. "You're brave."

"Really?" asked Edith, who had never been called brave before.

"Of course! Who else would dig up a grave at two in the morning?"

"Well, just let me rest for a second," said Edith. And without even stopping to think, she sat down hard—right on the wet and dirty coffin.

Without warning, the lid gave way, cracking in two, and Edith went tumbling right into the coffin.

There *was* something in it, something too horrible to imagine. It felt like a body. In the brief moment she touched it, before she leapt to her feet shrieking, she felt clothing—a man's suit—with something inside it.

"It's Mike!" howled Edith, pressing herself against the far side of the sodden pit. "I just sat on a corpse!"

But Timothy was laughing. "Take a second look," he said.

A flash of lightning illuminated the scene momentarily.

Edith forced herself to look down at the coffin again.

It was a man's suit, but Mike wasn't in it.

Timothy bent over and unbuttoned the jacket. Inside were pillowcases, and inside the pillowcases were a tea set, a platter, silverware, and some jewelry.

"Look at this!" cried Edith. "They robbed more people than just that old lady."

A moment later, Timothy looked up and whistled softly.

"What is it?" asked Edith.

"We're seven feet down," explained Timothy over the pelting drops, "and the rain has made the sides too slippery to hold on to. We can't get out."

"I know!" said Edith, starting to dig little pockets in the earth on the side of the grave. "We can dig toeholes."

"Watch out," warned Timothy, "or the soil could come tumbling down on top of us. We'd be buried alive."

Slowly, carefully, they started digging. It was cold, messy work, but finally they had dug enough toeholes to start climbing out.

Edith was lighter, so she went first.

I'll never be able to do this, she was thinking, but somehow she did. At last, her head was above ground level. Soon she was able to lean forward and pull herself along the rain-drenched grass, helped by a firm shove from Timothy.

She was dirty and wet, but she was out. It felt wonderful.

"I'll toss out the stuff," called Timothy, heaving up pillowcase after pillowcase. "Then we'd better get out of here before someone shows up."

"Boy," said Edith, "this must be worth a fortune!"

"Here comes another!" cried Timothy. "It's the last. Now, here I come!"

Timothy scaled the side of the open grave. His blond hair was plastered across his forehead and his face was streaked with dirt, rain, and sweat. Soon his head appeared above ground level, then his shoulders, then his waist.

"You're almost there," called Edith.

Timothy leaned forward and with a little help from Edith pulled himself out of the empty grave.

"I just wonder who's—" he began, but he never finished his sentence. At that moment the earth gave way.

Edith heard a sickening thud as Timothy fell back into the grave and hit the bottom hard. She rushed to the side of the hole. Peering in anxiously, she saw Timothy's dark form lying still at the bottom.

Back into the grave climbed Edith. A moment later, she cried out in relief. Timothy was still breathing.

Knowing she could never get him out by herself, Edith covered Timothy with the blanket that had been used in place of a shroud. It was fairly wet, of course, but at least it offered some protection.

Once again, Edith climbed out of the pit. It was harder, without Timothy's help, but at last she managed it.

She decided to take one pillowcase and run across the fields to Bluebird Hall.

Suddenly, a spine-tingling sound came from nowhere.

"Who's there?" cried Edith. "Who is it?"

"Who, who," came the mocking reply.

"Show yourself!" commanded Edith, suddenly feeling brave.

A second later she had to laugh. Down through the darkness swooped the owl, hooting as she flew. She landed on Edith's shoulder and seemed to be pointing with her head. She was gesturing in the direction away from Bluebird Hall.

"Maybe Ruth will help us," Edith said to the owl. "It's worth taking the time to find out if she's there."

But the owl was heading away from Bluebird Hall and the fields, and toward the thick surrounding woods. She would fly a few feet and then look back at Edith, a fierce glow illuminating her wise eyes.

Edith ignored her. Through the night she ran, the pillowcase filled with silver under one arm. The rain was coming down even harder now, and Edith ran with her head bowed.

After running a few feet, she stopped to call for the owl. "I don't care what you think," she shouted, "I'm going to Bluebird Hall!"

"That's what you think," cried a gruff voice.

"You can talk!" marveled Edith. "That's—"

"Of course I can talk," said the voice. The next thing Edith knew, a rough hand was covering her mouth so she couldn't scream while another one was holding her so she couldn't run.

It was Mark, along with Hugh and three other men Edith didn't know by name.

"Look at this," said Mark while Edith struggled. "She's gone and stolen our silver!"

"She didn't get much," said Hugh. "But I still don't like it."

Edith struggled and tried to scream.

"She's wriggling like an eel," sneered Mark.

"Gag her," ordered Hugh, "while I tie her up."

In an instant, Edith was gagged and her hands were tied behind her back.

"What now?" asked Mark.

Hugh bowed his head in thought. "I say we take her to the boss," he said.

At least I'll find out who's behind this, thought Edith.

Through the rain and the dark, Mark and Hugh bundled Edith. The three others followed behind, checking to make sure they weren't being followed. They skirted Bluebird Hall and continued along the main road; it was so late, they met no one.

Before long they came to an elegant-looking house. It had a few lights still burning. Still dragging Edith, Mark and Hugh went around to the backdoor. The other men waited outside.

Just as they arrived, someone opened the door and stepped into the night. Edith's spirits fell to see it was Bertha, the Bearded Lady.

"Mark, Hugh," she said, "you're not supposed to be seen here. It might arouse suspicion."

"There's trouble," said Hugh, and shoved Edith forward. "We just caught her near the grave, and with some of the silver."

"Let the boss figure it out," said Bertha. "My part in this is over."

Mark and Hugh opened the door and shoved Edith into a dimly lit kitchen.

"What have we here?" cried a nasal voice from somewhere in the next room. It sounded familiar. When Edith saw and recognized the face that went along with the voice, she thought she should have known who it would be all along.

"Mr. Snivell," began Hugh, and soon he had told the man the story of their finding Edith.

"So," said Mr. Snivell, rubbing his hands together, "we have a little snoop. Are you sure she was alone?"

"Positive."

Behind her gag, Edith was keeping very quiet.

"Listen, boys," said Mr. Snivell, "put her up in the little room off the attic. I'll get the key so we can lock her in."

"Then what'll we do with her?"

"We'll figure out something," said Mr. Snivell in a nasty voice.

Edith found herself in a small room. Mark and Hugh tied her to a sturdy chair with her hands behind her back. They kept the gag on.

Then Mark and Hugh left and Mr. Snivell appeared with the key. "I don't like taking chances," he said to Edith. He examined her thoughtfully. "Smart girl," he said finally. "I'll say that for you. You figured out what we were up to, didn't you? I started that rumor about a ghost, of course. It was child's play faking those deaths. Mrs. Sheehan really believed the men had died."

Mr. Snivell smiled a narrow smile at his own ingenuity and then consulted his watch. "Greenvale was our last robbery," he said. "I needed a certain amount of money, you see. And now I have it—at least I will once I dig up all the silver and sell the whole lot of it. Perhaps you are wondering why I would need money," Mr. Snivell continued.

Edith squirmed unhappily.

"Those Byrams named an impossible price to buy Blue-bird Hall. The fools. They never thought I'd be able to raise that much money. But I have. Just think, this time next week, Bluebird Hall will be mine!"

Edith looked at Mr. Snivell in horror.

"Now, I must provide Mark and Hugh and the rest with dry clothes. I'm afraid I'm going to have to send them out in the rain again. They have to fill in the grave before morning. They'd better hurry, too. It wouldn't do for someone to peer out of a window and see my men digging in the family graveyard. Young woman," he concluded, "I am not known for my patience. I am keeping the gag on you so I shall not be disturbed. My lovely wife, Mabel, is at her sister's, so there is no one in the house to hear your screams, anyway. Now, I must be off. We shall deal with you—later. Enjoy your stay here at Snivell Manor!"

As soon as Mr. Snivell left, Edith tried screaming. She couldn't make a sound. She tried getting loose from the chair. She couldn't do that, either.

Mr. Snivell was sending Mark and Hugh to fill in the grave—and Timothy was lying at the bottom of it covered up and unconscious. And there was nothing Edith could do about it.

She was completely, utterly trapped.

It's all my fault! thought Edith miserably.

12

TRAPPED

Tied to a chair in a room three stories up. It was impossible. There was no way out.

There *is* a small window in the locked door, Edith thought desperately. But even if she broke the glass, the window would still be too narrow for her to squeeze through. And it was positioned so high in the door, she wouldn't be able to reach through it to the lock on the other side. She doubted Mr. Snivell would have left the key in the lock, anyway. He didn't seem like that kind of person.

Maybe they just won't fill in the grave without looking in it first, prayed Edith. But she didn't have much hope. Mr. Snivell had told the men to do the job quickly.

The sound of breaking glass interrupted Edith's unhappy thoughts.

Through the window came a flash of white. The owl circled the attic room, then landed on the floor next to Edith. Her yellow eyes examined the girl dolefully, and she shook her head as if in annoyance.

I know, thought Edith, I should have listened to you. I should have gone back into the woods. Then she shook her head. I can't believe I'm sitting here apologizing to an owl! In fact, I can hardly believe any of this! she thought.

Now the owl got to work. She tugged and pulled and bit at the ropes with her sharp beak. Once or twice, the owl's hooked beak pierced Edith's skin by mistake.

At last Edith was free. She removed the gag, then ran to the window. It was a sheer drop—no way out that way.

Edith tried the door. It was a good, thick one—impossible to break through. Again she eyed the small window in the door—she'd never fit through, never.

But someone else could.

Edith looked at the door, then at the owl. Yes, she could send the owl for help!

Edith reached into the pocket of her dress. Her pencil was still there, and a piece of paper, too. She would write a note. But to whom?

Time was passing. Mark, Hugh, and their companions could already have arrived at the grave by now. What would happen if Timothy were to die in the past? And what would happen to her, and to Tad, Martha, and Joe in the present?

"Tad, Martha, and Joe!" Edith repeated to herself. "That's it."

Without pausing to consider, Edith dashed off a note and gave it to the owl. Then, taking the ring from around her neck, she placed it on one of the owl's talons.

Edith pointed to the window in the door.

The owl took flight.

"Go!" cried Edith. "Hurry!"

Praying that it would work, Edith watched as the owl crashed through the glass, then vanished into thin air.

"It worked! It worked!" cried Edith.

Then an awful through struck her. Hadn't Tamburlaine said that someone couldn't go to the same place twice? Would that mean another person couldn't travel to that place?

"I'll be trapped here!" Edith gasped aloud. "If Joe, Martha, or Tad can't get here, I'll be stuck in the past—without the ring! I'll never get home!"

The owl passed through the years with the beat of a wing and soon alighted in Bluebird Hall.

Martha was still sitting by the phone, Tad was walking in small circles near the stone wall, trying to figure things out, and Joe was in the hallway near Edith's door.

A strange whistling sound suddenly came from Edith's room. Joe entered in time to see a white blur flash in front of his eyes. He looked again.

There on a bedpost sat the owl, examining him thoughtfully.

"Tamburlaine's owl!" cried Joe.

With great dignity, the owl put out one of her feet. There was the note, and there was the ring.

Joe grabbed them.

"It's got to be from Edith," Joe said to himself as he read the note. "I'm trapped in the past. Please help!" it began. "I'm being held prisoner in Snivell Manor, in a room off the attic. Something terrible will happen if I don't get out, and not just to me. Go to the room right away, and bring the ring with you. Hurry! Help!" It was signed "Edith."

"What room?" Joe wondered out loud. "Bluebird Hall is full of rooms. How am I supposed to know which one?"

Joe looked hopefully at the owl. The owl looked back at Joe. She blinked her eyes, then nodded toward the door of the room that wasn't there.

"That door doesn't go anywhere," Joe told the owl. "It just opens onto a blank wall."

The owl only nodded again toward the door.

"Maybe you mean the closets in the hall," said Joe and went out to investigate, leaving the owl shaking her head disdainfully.

"No luck there," said Joe returning.

This time the owl flew over and tapped her beak against the door.

"Okay, okay," said Joe. "I'll show you it doesn't go anywhere."

Joe opened the door. "See," he began, "it—"

Then he froze in his tracks. "Tamburlaine!" cried Joe as he stepped into the room and ran to hug his old friend.

"Joe," said Tamburlaine simply. "I knew we would meet again."

"But—" began Joe when Tamburlaine interrupted.

"Joe," he said, "I am glad you found your way here, for there is no time to lose. Edith—"

"I know," said Joe. "She's trapped at Mr. Snivell's and she sent for me to rescue her."

Tamburlaine nodded. "It might be dangerous, Joe," he said softly.

"I'm ready," said Joe. "Just wait a second while I go get Tad and Martha."

"Wait," said Tamburlaine. "You see, it might not be that easy to send you to where Edith is. In fact, it might not work at all. One person may not go to the same place twice. Now, for two people to go at different times to the same place, well, it may be possible, although extremely risky. I doubt the magic can send all three of you on this occasion. And besides, there is not much time—if it works at all."

"I'm willing," said Joe.

"I know you are. Before you go, let me tell you one thing: You will not have long to be there. If you do make it back to the past, you will be viewed by time as a sort of foreign body, and time will attempt to eject you back into the present. If that happens, you must leave immediately, bringing Edith and Timothy with you."

"How will I know it's happening? And who's Timothy?"

"Edith will explain who Timothy is. As for knowing, you *will* know. Now, you must go. There is not a moment to lose."

By this time, a door had appeared on the far wall of the room that wasn't there.

"But how will I know what to do?" asked Joe.

"I shall send a guide," said Tamburlaine. "The owl."

"But I thought—"

"I know, Joe, but she is a magic creature and can travel through time more easily than you or Edith. I believe she can manage one more trip with the help of the ring, but no more. Put on the ring and step through the door," instructed Tamburlaine. "Then, once you have arrived, remove the ring. Do not wear it again until you wish to return."

With the owl on his shoulder, Joe opened the door, stepped through, and vanished. The next second, he materialized on the staircase at Snivell Manor. He made his way up to the attic on tiptoe. The house was still. Dimly, from the floor below, Joe could hear someone snoring.

Joe tried door after door until he came to one that wouldn't open.

"Edith," he said softly, "are you in there?"

"Joe," called Edith. "Is that you?"

"Tamburlaine sent me, and the owl. He said we have to hurry."

"Can you get me out?"

Joe examined the door. "I'll need a screwdriver," he said, looking at the door's hinges.

"That might take too long," cried Edith. "Maybe you should—"

"Won't take a minute."

"Joe . . ." began Edith, but Joe was gone.

Silently, he made his way to the basement. Snivell Manor no longer existed in the present, but Joe could remember his father taking Tad, Martha, and him to see it just before the Snivells had had it razed. Joe recalled there had been a large basement with a number of workrooms—perfect places to find tools.

Joe passed the second floor. Mr. Snivell's snores were still echoing loudly.

Making his way through the darkness, Joe paused in the

kitchen to feel his way around on the counter. He was lucky: He found a candle and matches.

By candlelight, Joe found the basement door. He went down the stairs and into a workroom. Yes, there was a screwdriver, and a good sturdy one at that.

In three minutes' time, Joe had returned to the top floor and quietly removed the door from its hinges. The owl watched Joe at work, nodding her head approvingly.

Out rushed Edith from the small attic room, dressed in the old-fashioned clothes Rosamond had given her. She was mud-stained, dirt-streaked, and drenched—yet somehow she had never looked so attractive.

"Edith," began Joe, but his cousin gestured wildly.

"Tell me later, Joe," she whispered. "We've got to get out of here. You'll see why."

Edith and Joe sneaked out of Snivell Manor and made their way across the rain-soaked meadows, with the owl making small circles in the air above them.

"You know," said Joe when they had exchanged stories, "I thought something had happened to you. I just didn't know how to bring it up."

"And I really wanted to tell you," said Edith, "but I didn't know how to bring it up, either. And besides, I guess I was sort of trying to show off, by going on an adventure all by myself."

Bluebird Hall was lost in darkness as they hurried by. Soon they were approaching the Byram family graveyard.

The owl perched on the shoulder of Joe's white jacket as he and Edith peered out from behind a thick oak.

There were the five men: Mark, Hugh, and the other

three, all big and burly. To Edith's immense relief, they hadn't started filling in the grave. Timothy was still alive!

The men were busy arguing about who would do the shoveling.

"We'll have to scare them off somehow," said Edith in a low voice.

"They don't look too scarable," observed Joe. "Or too friendly."

Edith looked at Joe, then at the men, and then back at Joe.

"I have an idea," Edith said. "It just might work. Quick, give me your jacket."

Looking doubtful, Joe removed his jacket and gave it to Edith. Edith then gestured to the owl, which alighted gracefully on Edith's shoulder.

It seemed to Joe that Edith was whispering something to the owl. The owl even appeared to nod her head thoughtfully. Edith then laid Joe's jacket on the ground. The owl flew down, grabbed the hem of the jacket, and took off, flying through the darkness with the jacket hanging beneath her own body.

"She looks like a ghost," said Joe.

"That," said Edith, "is the idea."

Gathering speed, the owl flew right toward the group of men, giving a series of low hoots. She even sounded like a ghost.

"What was that?" asked one of the men nervously.

"Nothing," said Hugh. "Start shoveling."

"I thought I heard something, too," said a second man.

At that point the owl made another pass. The wind

from her swift flight extinguished the men's lantern, and in the darkness the owl looked more ghostlike than ever.

"*Whoo-whoo*," keened the owl as she flew, Joe's coat making her seem three times her normal size.

"It's a ghost!" cried one of the men as the owl floated past them and vanished.

"There's no such thing as ghosts," said Hugh, but he no longer sounded convinced. "Old man Snivell just made up that story," he added. "It isn't true."

"Well, it came true," said another man. "And I'm getting out of here before the ghost gets me!"

"Me, too," said the second. "Me, too," added the third.

Soon Mark and Hugh were standing alone.

The owl made yet another pass, crying mournfully.

"Fill in the grave yourself if you want to," said Mark. "I'm not hanging around in a haunted graveyard!"

Mark followed the three retreating men, leaving Hugh alone near the open grave.

"Hugh! Hugh!" cried Edith in a high, unrecognizable voice. "I am coming for you!"

That was too much even for Hugh. He turned tail and ran.

The men had been so frightened, they even left the stolen loot behind them.

13

A WHITE SHADOW

Carefully, Edith and Joe lifted Timothy out of the grave. He was now semiconscious, and was shivering terribly as they laid him gently on the wet grass. They covered him as best they could with Joe's jacket.

"We tied the horse and cart near Bluebird Hall," Edith told Joe. "We'll have to carry Timothy to it."

It was long, hard work, for Timothy was surprizingly heavy. Luckily, Joe was strong. Edith was amazed that she could keep up with him.

Dawn was breaking as they passed by Bluebird Hall, carrying their own grandfather, three-quarters of a century before they were even born!

They had just laid Timothy in the back of the cart when Edith had another idea. "Listen," she said, "I can take Timothy back to the circus by myself."

"You know how to drive a horse and cart?" asked Joe, incredulous.

"I can do it," said Edith. "Timothy showed me how. I think you'd better go back for the silver and bring it to the police station—quickly, before Snivell and his men come back. And make sure you tell the police about the other four fake graves so Snivell doesn't get his hands on the rest of the stolen silver. We have to be sure he can't buy Bluebird Hall."

"But won't the police wonder who I am?"

Edith smiled.

"Look at yourself," she said. "You and Timothy could be twins. Just tell them you're from the circus. They'll believe you, I'm sure. It will even explain your clothing. They'll just think it's some kind of circus costume."

Soon Edith and Timothy were heading off in the cart and Joe was heading back to the grave. They'd arranged to meet later at the circus in Greenvale.

"How'd it go?" asked Edith when Joe appeared by Timothy's bedside a few hours later.

"Great!" said Joe. "They believed I was Timothy, and they believed me about the fake graves and everything. They sent some men to dig them up that very minute. There's no way Snivell can get hold of any of it—and no way he can get the money to buy Bluebird Hall."

"Good work, Joe," said Edith.

"How's Grandfather?" asked Joe.

"Still asleep. I think he'll be fine. It was just a nasty crack on his head, but nothing's broken."

"When will you tell him who he is?"

Edith considered the question. "I'm going to wait until he's feeling well," she said. "And speaking of feeling well, Joe, you don't look so hot. You look pale."

"I do feel kind of strange," Joe admitted, leaning against the wall. "It's like—"

A soft groan from the bed interrupted them.

"Where am I?" asked Timothy in a dazed voice, trying to sit up in bed. "What happened?"

"I'll tell you all about it in a minute," said Edith. "And lots of other things, too. But first, there's someone I'd like you to meet. He's my cousin, Joe."

"He looks exactly like me!" said Timothy. Then his expression grew troubled. "I must be seeing things."

"No," said Edith, "Joe really does look exactly like you."

"That isn't what I meant. Look at him. Now I can see right through him."

Edith wheeled around. Joe was becoming steadily translucent. She could see the wall right through him.

"Edith," cried Joe, "I'm fading. I'm being pulled back. I can't fight it! He said this might happen. . . ."

For a moment Edith was stunned. Then she leapt into action.

"Hold on, Joe!" she cried. "You can't go without us! You have the ring!"

Joe was gasping for breath. He was becoming paler and paler; soon he would vanish altogether.

"Timothy," urged Edith. "You have to get out of bed." Using all her strength, she half helped, half dragged a wobbly Timothy to his feet. Joe now looked like a white shadow.

"Where's the ring?" Edith asked.

"In my pocket. Take it out for me. I don't have the strength."

Like the rest of him, Joe's pants pocket was becoming invisible. But Edith located it and found the ring.

Edith put it on.

"Timothy," she said, "I can take you home. Do you want to come with me?"

"Yes," said Timothy weakly.

Edith took hold of Timothy with one hand and Joe with the other. With all her strength, she pulled them toward the door. In a blind panic, Edith kicked open the door.

They were almost there.

All they had to do was step through. Timothy would be brought back to the room that wasn't there so Tamburlaine could return him to his proper place in time. Everything was going to be all right.

Lurching forward, Edith passed through the door, Joe on her left and Timothy on her right, the owl perched haphazardly on her shoulder.

Now followed the familiar sensations of moving rapidly and standing still at the same time, and of rising and falling and not moving at all. Through clouds of light and oceans of time they passed.

The next moment Edith found herself in the room that wasn't there. Joe lay at her feet, still in pain but becoming more solid by the second.

"We brought back Timothy!" Edith rejoiced.

"But he isn't here," said Joe.

"He has to be!" cried Edith. "He was with us."

Joe was right. Timothy was not there.

At this moment the wind sprang up in the shadowy room, a cold, bitter wind. The owl turned around slowly so the wind was at her back.

Joe clambered to his feet.

A gleam of warm light soon appeared on the room's outside wall. It quickly turned into a door—Tamburlaine's door.

Edith and Joe, along with the owl, were ushered into Tamburlaine's welcoming cabin. They sat by the fire, cups of tea pressed into their hands.

"Tamburlaine," wailed Edith, "what happened?"

"Edith," Tamburlaine said gently, "you did extremely well. You were very brave, very resourceful."

"But where's Timothy?"

Tamburlaine looked into Edith's eyes. It was then that she remembered.

"No!" she cried. "I forgot!"

"What did you forget?" asked Joe.

"We were supposed to surround Timothy for the voyage back. He should have been in the middle, not on the end!"

"That is so," said Tamburlaine solemnly. "You see, Joe, the voyage to the present was easier for Edith and you. You were returning to where you belong. The gap created by your departure was here, waiting to be filled. But for Timothy it was different. There is no gap for him here, so time would tend to repel him."

"But what happened to him?"

"He stepped for a moment into time but was pushed out so rapidly that he never even knew what had happened. All he will know is that he was suddenly alone."

"But can't we go back and get him?" cried Edith.

Tamburlaine shook his head.

"You know better than that, Edith," he said. "It cannot be done."

"But Joe came for me!" pleaded Edith. "Why couldn't Martha or Tad go back for Timothy?"

"Sending Joe was risky enough and nearly turned into a calamity. If Joe had vanished before you had taken the ring, you would have been trapped in the past. That place in the past is now closed to *anyone* from this period of time."

"Even the owl?"

"Even the owl."

Joe put his arm around his cousin. "You did your best, Edith," he said. "Next time . . . next time we'll bring him back."

"Joe is right," said Tamburlaine. "You did your best. You did not bring back Timothy, but perhaps he was not meant to return at that point. Perhaps you were sent to that time to accomplish something else."

"What did I accomplish?" asked Edith, despairing.

"Edith, you accomplished something very important. You stopped Horatio Snivell from amassing enough money to buy Bluebird Hall. Had you not done that in the past, in the present you would have returned to find that Bluebird Hall had become Snivell Manor."

"I guess we did pretty well then," said Joe.

"Very well," said Tamburlaine. "Joe, you were being pulled back by forces greater than you know. You did a masterful job of resisting."

"But I hardly resisted at all."

Tamburlaine shook his head and smiled. "You resisted

mightily," he said. "Someone else would have been swept back with the first wave. You held on long enough to bring Edith with you."

Joe bowed his head modestly. It was his first trip in time; he was thankful he had done well. He had a lot to tell Tad and Martha.

"I still can't believe that Timothy was actually here," said Edith, "here in Bluebird Hall, and I let him slip through my fingers. If only I'd told him who he was. What do we do now? How do we find where Timothy went next?"

"That you must discover for yourself. But you cannot return to places you have already been. And sending someone else — Tad or Martha — to a place already visited is much too dangerous."

"But we don't know what Timothy was planning to do next."

"You are a smart girl," said Tamburlaine. "You will find out."

"I hope you're right," said Edith in a low voice. "I hope you're right."

14
RESEARCH

They got back just in time for dinner.

Tad had left the stone wall and Martha the telephone to join their mother at the table. Their jaws dropped to see Joe and Edith enter together.

"Edith!" said Mrs. Byram. "What pretty clothes! Wherever did you get them?"

Edith suddenly realized she'd forgotten to change. "My clothes?" she said. "I . . ."

"Found them in the attic," interjected Joe. "That's where we've been since the afternoon, looking around in the attic."

"I was wondering where you got to," said Mrs. Byram as she served some salad. "You both seemed to vanish into thin air."

Tad examined his brother and cousin. No, there could be no doubt about it. They'd had an adventure. He could tell by the gleam in their eyes.

Martha, too, had figured it out. Her eyes were blazing dramatically, and she was getting her famous actress expression. "Selfish brats!" she hissed under her breath.

"There wasn't time to find you," said Joe.

"I wanted to," began Edith when Mrs. Byram interrupted.

"What on earth are you four talking about?" she demanded.

"Oh, nothing, Mom," said Martha. "Nothing at all."

Bluebird Hall was such a large house that it had three attics. Tad and Martha had chosen the smallest one as their private meeting room. Dinner was long over, and the twins had invited their brother and cousin to come to the small attic.

"All right," demanded Martha, "confess!"

Joe looked at Edith. Edith looked at Joe. They both nodded and out poured the story.

"Good grief!" exclaimed Tad. "That's incredible!"

Even Martha was impressed.

"Edith," she said, "I never knew you were so brave!"

Edith blushed happily.

But Tad's logical mind was pressing forward. "So that's why the photograph is fading! It's a warning: either we get Timothy back to his real path in life or—"

"Or we fade, too," said Joe gravely.

"Tad and I can go back to Sheehan's Circus—" started Martha.

"You can't," Edith interrupted. "None of us can go back to that place again. Remember what happened to Joe? I don't think Tamburlaine would let us risk our lives again."

Four heads were bowed in thought.

"Research," said Edith suddenly. "We'll have to do lots and lots of research."

"What do you mean?" asked Martha.

"I mean, we have to look in every old reference book, in every list, in every old newspaper—everywhere we can think of. Sooner or later Timothy's name will have to come up. Just remember, he thinks his last name is Thomas."

"I hate doing research," grumbled Martha.

"It's better than finding out we don't really exist," Tad reminded her.

"Tomorrow, then," said Joe. "We meet at the library at four o'clock. We'll stay there until it closes, and we won't give up until we find something."

"I'll spend the entire day there," offered Edith.

"What about that story you have to write?" Tad asked. "The one your mother's always bugging you about?"

"This seems much more important," said Edith. "As soon as we find Timothy, I'll do it. Anyway, it's not due for a little while yet."

"Okay," said Joe, "until tomorrow at four."

And the four Byrams shook hands.

It hasn't even been a whole day here, thought Edith as she climbed into bed that night, but it was two days there. No wonder I'm so tired.

Once or twice Edith woke briefly during the night, but she fell back into a deep sleep.

It was the light of morning that woke her.

Edith sat up in bed and her yawn turned into a scream.

Her bedroom was gone.

Her bed stood on a beautiful stretch of beach. White sand sloped down to the turquoise water of a peaceful ocean. Behind her, beyond the beach, were steep sand dunes. It was wonderfully quiet.

Edith stepped out of bed onto the sand. It was smooth and surprisingly cool to the touch. At the water's edge, low waves lapped against the shore. Edith saw white flowers floating on the water.

Suddenly, she felt a hand on her shoulder.

"Come walk with me," said Tamburlaine.

Down the long beach Edith strolled with a silent Tamburlaine.

"Tamburlaine," she said, "I'm . . . I'm sorry."

"Sorry for what?"

"I should have remembered how to bring Timothy back. I'm supposed to have such a good memory. I would have remembered if we hadn't left in such a rush. Maybe I stayed too long because I was having the best time of my whole life."

"Perhaps it was meant to be," suggested Tamburlaine. "Perhaps Timothy has work yet to accomplish in his other life."

As they walked on, Edith knelt down to pick up a perfect seashell, smooth and glowing. She put it to her ear and could hear the sea. "Tamburlaine, where are we?"

"That would be hard to explain. But I thought you needed a little rest after all the difficulties you faced on your journey. So I brought you here."

For a moment they stopped walking. Tamburlaine looked far out to sea, where white birds were circling.

Then they turned around, retracing their footsteps in the sand.

Soon they reached the spot where they'd started. Someone was in the water, swimming. It was Joe.

"May I go in the water?" asked Edith.

Tamburlaine nodded, and—nightgown and all—Edith waded into the beautiful ocean.

It was just the right temperature: not too warm, not too cool. The gentle swells lifted her up and down, and the white floating flowers scented the air. Edith couldn't remember feeling so peaceful and so happy. It was like a perfect dream.

When Edith awoke next, she was back in her bed, and her bed was back in her bedroom. So, she thought, it was a dream.

But at breakfast, Joe had a white, fragrant flower in the buttonhole of his shirt.

"He was there then, too," Edith whispered to herself. "It wasn't a dream after all."

Edith suddenly raced from the table, up to her room. There, in the pocket of her nightgown, she found the sea-shell. Putting it up to her ear, she heard the sighing of the beautiful sea.

They learned a lot at the library over the next three days, but not what they needed to know. They learned, for example, that Sheehan's Traveling Circus had closed soon after the fake deaths had been exposed. According to the newspaper reports, the Sheehans had tired of circus life and had decided to settle down. The four Byrams learned that the police chief received a lot of praise for discovering and returning the stolen items, although the actual culprit had never been captured. They also read, in a copy of the local newspaper, that the police chief and his wife took an extensive — and expensive — vacation shortly after solving the case.

"So," said Tad, "we can bet Mr. Snivell bribed him to keep quiet about who was behind it all."

"Those Snivells!" said Martha dramatically. "They are *always* bribing somebody!"

"But there is a good side to it," put in Joe. "Right, Edith?"

"Right," said Edith, catching on right away. "Whatever extra money Mr. Snivell had lying around had to be spent bribing the police chief, not putting down a deposit on Bluebird Hall."

By the end of those three days, their eyes were red with strain. The four of them had scoured local and national newspapers, membership files of old organizations, real estate records, marriage licenses — everything they could get hold of. But no mention of their grandfather had surfaced anywhere.

"He just seems to have vanished from the face of the earth," sighed Martha.

"And so might we if we don't find him and bring him back," said Joe.

"I used to think I was really good at research," said Edith. "I've just got to keep trying!"

"Speaking of trying," said Tad, "how's your story going?"

"I haven't even started," admitted Edith. "This seems so much more important."

114

"It is, but try explaining that to your mother!" said Tad. "She's expecting you to have it done and mailed off in a few days."

Mrs. Byram was serving Tad, Martha, and Joe an afternoon snack in Bluebird Hall's comfortable kitchen. They'd just come home and were grabbing a bite before heading out to join Edith at the library. Great-aunt Ruth had dropped in to see them.

"I've just received a note from Simon Andrews's housekeeper," she said. "It seems he so admired the painting I gave him that he's sent me one in return — one he thought I might especially like. I have yet to receive it —"

But Ruth never finished the sentence.

The kitchen door burst open and in darted Edith. She'd evidently been running. Her face was flushed and her eyes were lit with excitement. She looked a lot less like the pale girl who'd arrived at Bluebird Hall the week before and a lot more like Martha.

"I've got it!" Edith cried. "I found it at the library!"

"Goodness," said Mrs. Byram, "I never knew libraries were quite *that* exciting."

Great-aunt Ruth's wise old eyes opened wide.

"Edith's been working on a story," Mrs. Byram explained to Ruth. "It will help determine her placement in her new school. I guess she found something at the library to help her write it. Is that right, Edith?"

"Uh," said Edith, "sort of."

Ruth still seemed speechless, so Martha spoke. "Mom, can we take the rest of our snack and go upstairs with Edith? We want to see what she's been working on."

Off went Edith, accompanied by Tad, Martha, and Joe, leaving their mother and great-aunt still sitting in the kitchen.

"Isn't that nice," Mrs. Byram said to Ruth. "The four cousins are finally getting along!"

Great-aunt Ruth nodded her head vaguely. She hadn't heard a word Mrs. Byram had said. Now she knew for sure. What she had almost remembered, what she had long suspected, what the photograph of the circus had to suggest—it was true. Then—or so she hoped—all might yet be well.

"Tell us right away or I'll faint with suspense!" said Martha.

"And don't leave out any details," added Tad.

"Just tell us!" said Joe.

Edith produced some photocopies.

"They're from an old book at the library," she said. "A book of military records."

"Military what?" asked Martha.

"Military records," said Edith. "They tell who joined the army, where they went, and that kind of thing. I finally remembered Timothy might have ended up in the army. So I looked, and he did."

"We found him! We found him!" cried Martha.

"Edith found him," said Joe.

"That's what I meant," said Martha.

They were all seated on Edith's bed, pouring over the photocopies.

"Calm down, Marth," said Tad. "We're not out of the

woods yet. We still have to find him and bring him home."

"Let's see," said Joe, riffling through the papers. "Brian Thomas joined the army in 1942. It says here he was sent to London for training. I wonder what kind of training."

"Espionage, I bet," said Edith. "There was some kind of school for spies in London."

"Wow," said Joe. "Our own grandfather—a spy in the Second World War!"

"He's not our grandfather yet," put in Tad. "Not until we bring him back!"

"But at least we know where to find him, thanks to Edith," said Joe.

"So we're going to London!" said Martha happily. "I've always wanted to go there! It's got the best theater in the world. I'll feel right at home."

"I wonder if all four of us can go," Tad said.

"Of course we can," insisted Martha.

"Let's see," said Tad. "Nineteen forty-two. He'll be thirty-four years old. Joe and Edith last saw him when he was fifteen."

"Just think how surprised he'll be to see me again!" exclaimed Edith. "It'll be nineteen years later, and I'll still be the same age."

"Once he gets over the shock," said Joe.

"Remember," put in Tad, "he's already seen you two disappear into thin air."

"I remember all too well," said Edith, sighing, when Mrs. Byram knocked on the door and entered the room.

"Sorry to interrupt," she said, "but, Edith, your mother's on the phone."

"Poor Edith," said Martha. "Aunt Alida is such a pain. She probably wants a progress report on that dumb story."

That was precisely what Aunt Alida wanted. Furthermore, she wanted Mrs. Byram to look over what Edith had written so far. The only problem was that Edith hadn't written one word.

"I'm sorry, Edith," Mrs. Byram told her niece when they'd gotten off the phone, "but I promised your mother I'd make sure you got the paper finished and sent off."

"But it hardly even matters," pleaded Edith. "It's just to see which English class they put me in."

"I'm sorry," said Mrs. Byram. "Truly I am. Your mother does seem to be, well, overanxious about it. And I promise you, Edith, that when she picks you up, I will talk to her about it. But we promised your mother, and a promise is a promise. You've apparently not been working when you were up in your room or at the library. What you were doing I can't imagine. But from now on, you're going to have to do your work on the dining room table so I can keep an eye on you."

"But, Aunt Marg—"

"I'm sorry, Edith. That paper is due soon, and it has to be finished and mailed off or your mother will never allow you to visit Bluebird Hall again. We'll start right now," said Mrs. Byram as severely as she could. "Go fetch your paper and pen."

"Poor Edith!" said Martha after Mrs. Byram left the room.

"My father would never have been so unreasonable,"

said Edith. "It's so unfair he had to die. Oh, I do miss him," she added, trying not to cry.

Martha was right at her side, her arm around her cousin.

"I know just how you feel," she said gently. "We all do. We miss our dad, too."

"If only I could see him one more time." Edith sighed.

"I know how you feel," said Martha again, thinking of her own father. With Tamburlaine's help, she, Tad, and Joe *had* been able to see their father again. Joe had even been able to talk with him.

Her cousins ushered Edith down to the dining room. She had given them permission to go to London without her if they had to. There was no time to waste, especially if Timothy had joined the army. He could be in grave danger.

"Maybe we can wait until after dinner," said Joe hopefully, patting her shoulder.

"I hope so," said Edith unhappily, staring down at page after page of blank paper, as Joe led Tad and Martha to the room that wasn't there.

15

LONDON, 1942

"I am afraid there is no time to wait for Edith," said Tamburlaine as he led Joe, Tad, and Martha to his cabin. It had been a long time since Tad and Martha had seen him, and the twins had missed him. Even the owl appeared glad to see them.

Soon Tamburlaine spoke.

"Your grandfather is in London," he said, "and in great danger. You must hurry."

The three Byrams returned to the room that wasn't there. Joe put on the ring. Edith had given it to him. Martha and Tad each took one of Joe's hands and waited as a door appeared in the far wall. In another instant the three Byrams had stepped through, into the white light of time.

It was nighttime, but not a light was shining anywhere. Even a car rolling by had its headlights off. Not a streetlight was burning. Not a single light shone from a single window on the street where Tad, Martha, and Joe stood.

The men and women in the street rushed past.

The three Byrams followed the crowd along the sidewalk. They passed shops. These, too, had their lights extinguished.

"What's going on here?" demanded Martha.

Suddenly, a horrible wailing noise reverberated down the busy street. For a moment everyone froze. Then they all started running: Parents picked up children, younger people assisted the old.

The wailing grew louder. The people rushed faster, all headed in the same direction. There was a sign with a symbol on it and a staircase leading down, under the street. Tad, Martha, and Joe watched the people disappear down the dark stairway.

"I think I know what's going on here," began Tad when a woman who had just rushed past them toward the stairway stopped and looked back. Seeing the puzzled looks on their faces, the woman retraced her footsteps and soon was standing next to them.

"Come on, loves," she said. "The siren's sounding. You must come to the shelter where you'll be safe. Lost your mum, I warrant. Don't fret, dears, I'll mind you till the all clear."

The Byrams let themselves be guided along the pavement and down the stairway.

At the bottom of the stairs, a passage led to a large, cavernous room filled with people. Some were lying on cots, others were sitting on blankets on the floor. Mothers rocked babies, while groups of men sat chatting in low voices.

"What's going on?" asked Martha.

"Just another air raid," explained the woman who was shepherding them. "Those dreadful bombs got my sister's house only last night. Thank goodness she was in a shelter. . . ."

"Good grief!" said Tad.

Joe looked grim. "We came here to keep our grandfather out of danger, and look where we end up."

"Did you say you were out looking for your grandfather?" asked the woman.

Ignoring Tad's and Joe's warning gestures, Martha replied, "That's right. Our grandfather's in the army."

The woman gave Martha a troubled look.

"Men the age of grandfathers are usually too old to be in the army," she said.

"Oh, I know that," said Martha. "But our grandfather's only thirty-four years old."

"I see," said the woman. It was clear that she thought Martha had gone crazy with fear.

Half an hour later the all clear sounded, and the people in the shelter slowly gathered their belongings and headed back to their homes.

"Now listen," said the woman to Tad, Martha, and Joe. "My name is Claire Bellerby, and I want you to come home to my flat until you're feeling better. I shan't take no for an answer. I'll make you a nice cup of tea and you can chat with my son—pray he's all right."

After a quick conference, the three Byrams decided to go with Mrs. Bellerby. "She found us for a reason," said Joe. "I'm sure. But we won't know what it is unless we go with her."

Mrs. Bellerby led the Byrams to a small apartment in London's East End, the poorest part of the city. On the way, they passed many bombed-out buildings. Mrs. Bellerby seemed to know the name of a person or a family in nearly every building they passed. Many a friend had been killed by the bombs. Others had fled London, and still more had moved in with neighbors.

"I've got four youngsters myself," Mrs. Bellerby told them. "The youngest three are in Wales for the duration, away from the range of the bombs. Only my eldest is with me. Evan. He refused to go.

"Everything is rationed," Mrs. Bellerby explained as she set out the tea things in her apartment, "otherwise I'd be giving you more."

"I wish I'd known about that," said Martha. "I would have brought some food with me."

Mrs. Bellerby gave Martha another strange look. She seemed to think Martha was in a state of shock.

"Now, loves," said Mrs. Bellerby, "do you know how you got here?"

"Not exactly," said Joe. "We're not from London, you see."

"Yes," said Mrs. Bellerby, "your accent isn't English. But why are you in London? You can't really be looking for your grandfather."

"We don't know," said Joe. He disliked lying, but he knew Mrs. Bellerby would never believe the truth. "You see, that's just the trouble: None of us can remember who we are or why we're here. I think we have amnesia. All we can remember are our first names."

"Amnesia," repeated Mrs. Bellerby, "and all three of you, too. Isn't that rather unusual?"

"Extremely," said Tad in his best scientific voice.

"Well," said Mrs. Bellerby, "perhaps you all got so frightened being caught in an air raid without your mum or dad, you just forgot everything. Here, dears, some tea will restore your memories. If not, we'll just pop you 'round to the police station. They'll know what to do."

"Oh," said Joe, "I'm sure we'll remember without being brought to the police."

"By the way," asked Martha, "it is 1942, isn't it?"

"Of course," said Mrs. Bellerby, giving Martha yet another odd look.

"What day of the week is it?" asked Tad.

"Goodness," said Mrs. Bellerby, "you *have* lost your memories! It's Saturday."

"Saturday," said Tad. "That means that officer training place will be shut tomorrow."

"Whatever are you talking about?" asked Mrs. Bellerby.

"Oh, don't mind him," explained Joe. "He's just talking to himself."

A friendly boy around twelve years old brought in three cups of tea the next morning. Tad, Martha, and Joe were camped out in Mrs. Bellerby's small sitting room.

"You three certainly sleep soundly," said the boy with a smile. "Mum said you looked as though you'd traveled three thousand miles in a single afternoon. I'm Evan," continued the boy. "I was at my uncle's when you and Mum got home. Mum's gone to work. She's a char."

124

"A what?" asked Martha, sipping her tea.

"A charlady—she cleans offices. Anyway, how about a spot of breakfast?"

"Sounds great!" said Tad and Joe at once.

"You know what," said Evan over breakfast, "you sound like Yanks."

"Like what?"

"Yanks—Americans. Are you?"

"Yes," admitted Joe. "We are."

"Then what are you doing here?"

"I'm afraid we can't remember," Joe said.

"Well, don't fret," said Evan. "You probably almost got hit by a bomb, and it knocked you silly for a bit. It happened to our neighbor's son. They found him wandering down Shaftesbury Avenue, and he couldn't even remember his own name."

"Then what happened?"

"His memory came back gradually, and he was able to tell the bobby his name and address."

"What's a bobby?"

"A copper. A policeman."

"Oh," said Joe. "Well then," he continued, "I bet our memories will come back, too. So if we leave suddenly, don't be worried. It'll mean we just remembered who we are and we went back home."

"Mum told me to take you over to the police station this afternoon. Perhaps your parents have reported you missing."

"I doubt it," said Martha. "Our mother probably hasn't even noticed we've gone."

"Don't be daft—" began Evan, but he never completed the sentence.

Like a shriek of pain, the air-raid siren called out its warning.

"Quick!" cried Evan. "To the shelter! The bombers are coming! Hurry or we'll be caught in the open!"

16
SABOTAGE

By the time Tad, Martha, Joe, and Evan had reached the street, the all clear had sounded.

"A false alarm," said Evan.

Martha looked around her at the many bombed-out buildings and shuddered. "Isn't it awful," she asked, "living like this—always scared of being killed?"

Evan gave the question some thought. "It *is* rather terrible," he said, "but all of us are in it together, from the king and the queen to Mum and me. They haven't left London, you know. Anyway," Evan continued, "what say you come with me to the factory?"

"Factory?" said Martha. "Don't you go to school?"

Evan gave a little snort. "It's Sunday," he said. "I go help out at the factory, sweeping up and that sort of thing. Just doing my bit."

"What do you manufacture there?" asked Tad as they headed off, passing yet another bombed-out building.

"We make crucibles," explained Evan. "Big vats that

are used to melt metal in. It's war work. Mum works there two nights a week."

"Must be hard," said Joe.

"It is, rather," said Evan, "but the worst of it is that it's so close to the river."

"You mean it gets flooded," said Tad.

"No, not flooded, although it does get frightfully damp. It's the rats I hate."

"Rats!" cried Martha. "Gross!"

"All cities have rats," said Evan, "but they usually stay hidden, deep down in basements. But so much of this area has been bombed, the rats have been dislocated—like the people, I guess. And they head down toward the river. People have been asked to bring down their cats. One large warehouse actually brought in a mongoose."

"I've never been in a war before," Joe told Evan.

"Neither had I," said Evan, "until now."

"Well, hullo, Evan," said a portly man in a vest. "Who are your friends?"

"Hello, Mr. Murrell," said Evan. "Meet Tad, Martha, and Joe, three Americans Mum found. This is Mr. Murrell, the manager of the factory."

"I've just taken on a Yank as my assistant," said Mr. Murrell after introductions had been completed. "Jolly good chap. Perhaps your three friends would like to meet him, Evan."

By the time Mr. Murrell produced the American, Joe and Evan had wandered off.

"It's good to meet some other Americans," said a friendly man with dark brown hair, a bushy beard, and thick glasses. "Hank's the name, Hank Jones."

"I'm Tad and this is my sister, Martha. Our brother's over there getting a tour of the factory. He's keen on machines."

Hank examined Joe with interest. And from across the factory floor, Joe examined the American. He looked strangely familiar.

Evan was just starting in on another machine when Joe looked over at his brother and sister. Suddenly, he saw Tad's expression change. Very discreetly, Tad elbowed Martha and nodded. Martha took the cue. Without warning, she began gasping for breath. Anyone who didn't know what an actress she was would think she had been taken seriously ill.

"My word," said Evan, "something appears to be wrong with your sister."

"I can't breathe!" Martha wheezed loudly. "It must be the rats. I'm allergic to rats."

"Let's take her outside," said Tad as a concerned Hank returned to his work.

"Are you feeling—" began Evan as soon as they'd helped Martha outside.

"Never felt better," said Martha, interrupting him. "Tell 'em, Tad."

"He's no American," burst out Tad. "No way. He said he was from New York City. But he isn't. I've been there, only I didn't tell him that. He said he lived on Eightieth Street. So, I asked which avenue he lived near—'Like on the corner of Eightieth and Sixth,' I said. And he said yes."

"So what?" asked Evan.

"So, that would mean he lived in a tree, right in the middle of Central Park. Sixth Avenue doesn't go up that far."

Evan gave the three Byrams a thoughtful look. "So," he said, "none of you really has amnesia."

"Evan," said Joe, "we did lie. But we had to. If we'd told the truth, you wouldn't have believed it. No one would."

"But we're telling you the truth now," said Tad. "Hank Jones is a phony."

Evan's alert brown eyes looked hard at the Byrams. "I believe you," he finally said. "Can't say just why, but I do. So, he could be a Nazi spy sent here to sabotage the factory."

"And don't look now," said Tad in a low voice, "but he's standing at the door of the factory, and he's staring at us. And hard, too. He must know we're on to him."

"Shall we tell Mr. Murrell?" asked Martha.

"Not without proof," said Evan, "that wouldn't be right."

"I know!" said Martha. "We'll trail him, the way they do in the movies!"

They didn't have long to wait.

Twenty minutes later they saw Hank leave the factory, walking briskly and carrying a large envelope under his arm. Darting along behind him, Evan and the Byrams followed at a discreet distance.

"Just look at that," said Evan. Hank had paused on a street corner and was looking at his watch. "He's waiting for someone."

"Spies are always meeting people," said Martha.

"And what better place than a very public street corner," said Tad. "No one would suspect anything."

"I don't know," said Joe. "He looks honest to me."

Hank seemed to be growing impatient. He kept examining his watch. At that moment, a man approached, looking at him uncertainly. Hank said something, the man nodded, and Hank handed him the envelope. The man walked off in one direction and Hank in the other.

Down a busy avenue went Hank, walking quickly. Tad thought he looked nervous.

Without warning, Hank stopped and backtracked a few steps. After examining some nameplates posted next to a door, he entered the doorway and disappeared up a dark staircase.

The next moment, Evan and the Byrams arrived at the door. Martha read the names aloud: "Matthews, 1-A; Denny, 1-B; Thompson, 2-A; Schmidt, 2-B."

"Schmidt!" said Evan. "That's a German name!"

Up the stairs they tore, not pausing until they stood stock-still outside 2-B. By pressing their ears against the door, they could just hear the voices inside.

". . . I got away as soon as I could," they heard Hank say.

"Thank you," the other voice replied. It sounded like an elderly man. "This information will be most helpful. Now, I think you should go."

"Good-bye for now," said Hank.

"*Auf Wiedersehen*," replied the man as Evan and the Byrams scattered.

"The danger you might have been in, you children!" said Mrs. Bellerby. "I don't even like to think about it!

What if the man is dangerous? What if he had turned around and seen you? It chills my blood."

"But what will we do?" asked Evan.

"Nothing," said Mrs. Bellerby. "You four have been up to quite enough for one morning, thank you very much. I shall consult with Mr. Murrell. He'll know what to do. And when I return, we must take our guests 'round to the police station. Doubtless, their parents are half mad with worry by now."

An hour later, Mrs. Bellerby returned. She was laughing to herself as she entered the small apartment. "I'm afraid your Nazi spy is nothing but a decent young American chap. Mr. Murrell gave him that envelope to give to someone Mr. Jones didn't know. And the German he went to see is an eighty-seven-year-old man who has lived in England for close to half a century. Mr. Jones was delivering some information about how he might receive some government assistance — nothing sinister there."

"But he gave Tad and Martha an address right in the middle of a park," argued Evan.

"He thought you said *Eighteenth* and Sixth."

"Good grief," said Tad, suddenly feeling very silly. "I guess we made a little mistake."

"Fortunately," Mrs. Bellerby continued, "Mr. Jones took no offense. He said he was glad to know American youth were so alert and so willing to take risks for their country. In fact, he seemed especially interested in you three Yanks. He even asked—"

"Mrs. Bellerby! Mrs. Bellerby!" An excited voice at the door interrupted Evan's mother in midsentence.

132

"The door's open," said Mrs. Bellerby.

In rushed a disheveled-looking woman.

"It's my sister," she said. "Her time's come. I need help getting her to hospital."

"I'm on my way," said Mrs. Bellerby, putting her coat back on. "Oh, Evan," she said, "I forgot to tell you. Mrs. Denton upstairs asked if you could sit with her children. She has to go out for an hour or so. She'll need you around nine tonight. I hope that's all right."

Then, turning to the Byrams, she added, "Now, listen, you three. You stay put until I return. It might be a while. I don't want you chasing about London, digging up trouble. I want you at home, out of harm's way. Then, when I get back, it's off to the police station. Agreed?"

"Agreed," said Evan, Tad, Martha, and Joe, sighing.

Mrs. Bellerby left. And, at nearly the same moment, German bombers were also departing, heading into the sky and flying northwest toward their target—the city of London.

17
UNDER COVER OF DARKNESS

"Well," said Joe, "I guess that's all cleared up."

"*Too* cleared up," said Martha suspiciously.

"Meaning what?" asked Tad.

"Meaning, aren't all Hank's explanations a little too convenient? He just *happened* to be seeing an old man who speaks German; he just *happened* to hear you say 'eightieth' in a way that sounded like 'eighteenth'; and he just *happened* to be staring at us like he'd never seen kids before. I don't believe any of it. Listen," Martha went on, "we can't do anything about Timothy until tomorrow, right? So maybe we were sent here on a Sunday to catch a cold-blooded spy."

"I see," said Joe, "sort of the way Edith and I stopped Mr. Snivell from amassing enough money to buy Bluebird Hall in 1923."

"What are you talking about?" asked Evan.

"Just some family stuff," explained Joe. "It's kind of complicated."

"So," Martha continued, "it's up to us and us alone to trap this evil agent. Are we all in it together?"

134

"Yes," said Tad and Joe.

"I guess so," said Evan.

"Good," said Martha. "Now let's think of a plan."

"I wish Edith were here," said Joe. "She's good at this sort of thing."

"I've got it!" said Tad finally. "We'll send Hank a note saying we're on to him and he'd better come talk to us or we'll go to the authorities."

"Better not have him come to the flat," said Evan.

"Where else could we meet him, Evan?" asked Joe. "We don't know London at all."

Evan considered. "About ten minutes' walk from here," he said, "there's a street that's entirely bombed-out. It would be a private place to meet."

"Good," said Martha, "let's say we'll be waiting for him. If he's really innocent, he'll think we're a bunch of crazy kids. But if he's really guilty, then he'll come. And there'll be just one of him but all of us."

"What time should we ask him to meet us?" asked Tad.

"I'm afraid it should be nine o'clock," said Evan. "That's when I have to baby-sit. But, you see, I overheard Mr. Murrell ask Hank to mind the phone until eight-thirty. That's when the factory closes on Sunday nights, so I know he wouldn't be free to meet us until nine. But that means I can't be there. And it means it would be after dark."

"Why is everyone so afraid of the dark?" said Martha.

"The air raids, of course. Nights are the worst. They come darting in over the channel under cover of darkness. That's why we have the blackout."

"The what?"

"The blackout—not a light can be showing anywhere. It makes London a harder target to find."

"So that's why it was so dark when we arrived," said Martha as Evan went to get pen and paper to write the note.

"He's got a mail slot at the factory," said Evan. "I happened to notice it when we were there. We'll leave it for him in his slot."

"But will he get it today?" asked Tad. "What if he leaves for the night without checking?"

"Oh, he'll get it," said Evan. "Mr. Murrell told me that Hank sleeps on a cot in a back room. Hank couldn't find lodging anywhere."

"More likely he wants to be alone there so he can wreck the machines or something," Martha speculated darkly.

Soon the note was delivered to the factory. The three Byrams and Evan pounded loudly on the door before leaving, hoping to attract Hank's attention. Then they made their way to the road Evan had described. They arrived at the bombed-out road a bit after eight o'clock.

"I should hate to be caught on a street like this!" Evan shuddered. "It's almost entirely bombed-out. There'd be no shelter at all if a raid should start. The best you could find would be the shell of a bombed-out building."

Martha shivered. "This road," she said. "It's like a wasteland."

"Thanks to the German bombing," said Evan.

Soon it was time for Evan to go. He went home regretfully, after imploring the Byrams to be careful.

"Good-bye, Evan," they called, "and thank you."

"Good-bye," replied Evan. "See you later at the flat."

"Yes," they said, "see you later." But they never saw him again.

"What was that?" said Joe a while later.

"What was what?" asked the twins.

"That . . . it sounded like footsteps."

Three sets of eyes peered down the dark street and saw a man approaching. He was the only person on the street. It was Hank.

"I told you," whispered Martha. "He *is* a spy!"

Slowly Hank approached them. He looked neither guilty nor angry, simply curious.

"I got your note," he said, looking only at Joe. "I am no German spy," he continued, "but I came because there was something *I* had to find out."

"How do we know?" demanded Martha.

Hank smiled. To Joe it was a familiar smile.

"I *am* an American," said Hank, "though not from New York, as you figured out. I am not permitted to tell where I really come from."

"Why not?" asked Tad.

"Because," said Hank, "while I am not a German spy, I *am* an American spy, which I tell you in dead secret. I was sent to keep watch at the factory."

"Then what was it you came to find out?" asked Tad. Hank seemed so forthright, it was impossible to doubt his word.

"It involves Joe," he said simply. "It makes no sense, Joe, but I recognize you. Do you recognize me?"

137

"You do look a lot like someone I met one time," Joe replied. "He was only fifteen years old then. I didn't see him for very long, and he was pretty dazed at the time. But he was blond and didn't wear glasses."

Hank smiled. "Disguises," he explained, removing them both.

With the thick glasses gone, Joe could look deeply into Hank's eyes, and all doubt was removed.

"Then . . ." began Joe, "you're Brian Thomas—or rather, Timothy."

Timothy smiled again. "You see, we were concerned someone might recognize me, so it was decided I should alter my appearance."

"I recognized you," said Joe, still staring. It was odd to see Timothy suddenly nineteen years older than he'd been the last time they'd met, only a few days before.

Timothy meanwhile was looking hard at Joe.

"Then you are indeed the same boy I saw when I was a lad, back at Sheehan's Traveling Circus with your cousin, Edith."

"I am."

Timothy leaned closer to Joe, examining him in the darkness.

"But you haven't aged a day," he said, amazed. Then, searching his memory, he said, "It's been nearly twenty years since you and Edith vanished. I could only imagine it had something to do with whatever it was that Edith never got to tell me. I have wondered what it was all this time."

"I can tell you now. But first, here's my brother and sister, Tad and Martha. This might sound strange, but—"

"What's that?" interrupted Tad. "It sounds like a low humming noise."

"Pray it's not—" Timothy began when the air-raid sirens started wailing.

"Good grief!" cried Tad. "It's bombers! And we're caught in the open."

"What do we do?" asked Martha. "Run for it?"

"No time," said Timothy. "They're really close. You can hear it. No, see over there? It's the shell of a big building. Come on, run. *Run!*"

The bombed-out shell stood halfway down the dark block, and soon Timothy had hurried the three Byrams through the remains of a doorway and into the building. It really was just a shell: There were tall walls on four sides, a few large crossbeams still in place, and an odd stick of smashed furniture here and there.

"Wouldn't we be safer in the street?" asked Tad.

"Probably not," said Timothy. "All sorts of sharp fragments go flying when a bomb hits. I've seen them go right through wooden doors. At least we're a bit safer behind these thick walls."

Martha looked up uncertainly to the dark sky above. What happens if I die here? she was wondering when the whine grew louder and louder, closer and closer.

Tad was trying to remember the safest position to be in when a bomb fell. Joe was nervously twisting the ring.

"Kneel down and cover your faces!" yelled Timothy as the whine and roar seemed to be passing directly overhead.

"Timothy—" began Joe, but he never finished the sentence.

It was then that the bomb fell.

It was an earthquake, a tidal wave, and a volcano all wrapped up in one. The bomb landed in the street, right where they'd been standing a minute before. It hit with such impact that it created a vast crater. It also caused part of the shell of the building to crash down as the force of the explosion sent the four of them flying.

It was over in a second.

Somehow, Tad, Martha, and Joe were thrown together in a heap up against one of the building's remaining inner walls.

For a moment they were in shock.

Martha screamed, "Timothy, Timothy," but there was no answer.

Then another crash sounded a few roads distant, and they saw the sky light up with flames. Another bomb had fallen, but this one had started a fire. People would go there first to help out. No one would come here to help them.

"Timothy!" they howled, but all they heard were screams and sirens and the fading whine of the planes. Searchlights crisscrossed the sky, shedding some light for their search.

Most of the shell of the building had crumbled, ending up right where they'd been standing before the impact of the bomb sent them flying.

Then Joe saw something. On top of a large heap of bricks and stone, a form was lying. And it lay under a thick beam that had somehow fallen across it. It was Timothy, and he wasn't moving.

Joe scrambled up the mountain of bricks and stone, followed by Tad and Martha. Timothy was barely conscious.

Frantically, Joe, Martha, and Tad tried moving the beam off Timothy's chest, but it was too heavy to budge even an inch.

Timothy was moaning and fighting for air.

At first Tad was too upset to think. And it didn't help much having Martha repeat over and over, "It's all my fault! I'm the one who thought he was a spy. We were supposed to bring him home, not lure him out to where a bomb would fall on him!"

"I've got it!" said Tad finally, and he set to work pulling bricks and stones from beneath Timothy's body. Gradually, he created a slight hollow, so they could pull Timothy out instead of trying to move the beam. If they were careful and only moved the bricks right beneath Timothy, the beam would stay where it was.

It was hard work, made harder by the darkness and the dreadful sound of Timothy's labored efforts to breathe.

The three Byrams cleared a small space and tried pulling Timothy out.

He didn't budge.

They pulled harder, yanking on Timothy's legs like a rope in a tug-of-war. Then they tried something Joe thought of: Tad grabbed both of Timothy's feet; Joe grabbed Tad by the waist; and Martha, at the rear, grabbed hold of Joe.

There in the darkness, surrounded by rubble, with all

their strength and then some, Tad, Martha, and Joe pulled, leaning back sharply on top of the hill of brick and stone. Surrounded by the remaining shell of the building that could collapse at any moment, they pulled harder and harder.

Then suddenly, Timothy came free, and Joe, Tad, and Martha were sent flying into the air, off the pile of rubble.

They fell backward together in a heap, still holding on to one another.

They didn't see it, but there it was in the darkness. It was the remains of the building's doorway, but it was still a door. And Joe had put on the ring to keep from losing it.

The three Byrams fell through the doorway.

Timothy, now free, looked in their direction just in time to see them vanish into thin air.

18

ANOTHER DOOR

For an instant they didn't know where they were. Then they recognized the field behind Bluebird Hall.

Rising to their feet, Tad, Martha, and Joe realized they were sore all over. Their fingers were bleeding from digging through the rubble. Looking at one another, they saw dirty, grimy faces and torn clothing.

"At least we saved Timothy," said Joe.

"But we're the ones who got him into trouble in the first place!" said Martha, trying to shake some London dirt and dust off her clothes.

"And we didn't bring him back with us," added Tad. "We failed again."

"That's the second time he's seen me vanish," Joe was saying as they left the field and entered Bluebird Hall.

A horrified shriek interrupted him.

"Joseph! Tad! Martha! Merciful heavens, what happened to you? You're all dirty and you're bleeding, too! Edith and I have been sitting in the living room, and we never even saw you go down the stairs. What happened?"

Martha tried to think fast. Luckily, her dramatic abilities also extended to the swift invention of excuses. "I was leaning out the window to admire the view when I . . . I lost my balance. And I tried to hold on to the windowsill with my fingers — that's why they got all bloody. Then Tad tried to grab me, and the same thing happened to him. Then Joe tried to grab both of us. But he couldn't. So we fell. All of us."

"I thought I heard a thud," said Mrs. Byram. "But, children, you could have been seriously injured. Are you sure you're all right?"

"We're fine," said Joe, "honestly, but we'd better go upstairs and change."

"Can Edith stop working for a minute and help us get cleaned up?" asked Martha.

"Of course," said Mrs. Byram. "Can I get you anything?"

"You know," said Joe, "I'd love a cup of tea."

"Tea?" said Mrs. Byram. "You never drink tea. What on earth is going on?"

"I doubt you'll ever know," said Joe under his breath as he, Tad, Martha, and Edith headed up to Edith's room.

"I bet Tamburlaine will be really mad at us," said Martha after they'd told Edith what happened. "And it's all my fault, I just know it is."

"I am not angry at all," said a voice from the doorway to the room that wasn't there. "Go to the mirror and take a look."

The four Byrams looked in the mirror on the wall near the bureau. Soon their reflections were replaced by an image.

"That's the factory!" cried Joe. "Where we met Timothy."

"Correct," said Tamburlaine. "It is the factory on the very night when you lured Timothy to the bombed-out building."

There was the factory, standing silent and dark in the London night. Then came a violent explosion, and suddenly the factory burst into flame and exploded. When the smoke cleared, not a brick of the factory was left standing. It was destroyed utterly.

"Good grief!" said Tad. "It's a good thing it was a Sunday night, otherwise lots of people could have been killed. Remember, the factory was shut on Sunday evenings."

Tamburlaine gave a thoughtful smile. "Remember, too," he said, "that Timothy was living in that factory. Had you not lured him out that evening, he would have been inside the factory when the bomb hit. He would not have survived."

"That means we *saved* his life!" said Joe.

"Thanks to me!" said Martha proudly. "It was all my idea, remember?"

"Was Timothy all right?" asked Joe.

"He was stunned and shaken," said Tamburlaine, "but had something happened to him, I would know."

"Now what do we do?" said Tad.

"This you must try to figure out for yourselves," said Tamburlaine as he entered the room that wasn't there and vanished through the door that glowed in the outer wall.

While Edith spent the days impatiently writing and rewriting her story, Tad, Martha, and Joe spent every spare moment at the library. They consulted every reference book, every old phone book, and every computer printout they could get their hands on.

"He's just vanished again," Martha told Edith two nights later. Edith had finally finished her story, retyped it neatly, and sent it off on the last day possible.

"There's no mention of him after London, no mention at all. Nothing. We even phoned Army Records in Washington," added Joe, "but they had no listing for a Hank Jones, or a Timothy Thomas, or a Brian Thomas, or a Timothy Byram, or anyone."

"It's a complete dead-end," said Tad, shaking his head.

"If only we hadn't lost hold of him in London," said Martha. "We saved his life, but we could end up losing ours."

"Don't I know it," said Tad. Without a word he pulled Great-aunt Ruth's replacement photograph out of an envelope. The four cousins examined it in silence.

Now they could see right through the figures to the scenery behind.

"It's as though we're not there at all," said Tad. "It's as though Great-aunt Ruth had just taken a photograph of the lawn."

"Oh, Edith," cried Martha, "you don't know how lucky you are not to have been in this picture!"

"But whatever happens to us will happen to Edith, too," said Joe.

"I know that," said Martha, "but at least she doesn't have to watch herself vanish away into nothingness."

"That's where you're wrong," said Edith. "Just look. This is the photograph I took of myself when I was in Boston."

Joe, Tad, and Martha examined the photo. Edith was fading to gray, and the alley where she was sitting was starting to show right through her.

"Tamburlaine will help us," said Edith. "He's got to now."

"He'd better," said Martha. "No one else can."

Tamburlaine listened to them, a serious expression clouding his face. He had been waiting for them in the room that wasn't there, a cool wind rustling his black hair. He always seemed to know when they really needed him.

Now they were all gathered around the fireplace in his cabin. The white owl was perched on Edith's shoulder and the fox was curled up in Tad's lap.

"Are you sure?" Tamburlaine asked, "that no further trace of Timothy exists anywhere?"

"We're sure," said Joe. "Believe me, we looked."

"I believe you," said Tamburlaine. "I was concerned that this might happen. And now it has."

"If only we'd held on tighter in London!" said Martha unhappily.

"Martha," said Tamburlaine, "I can only say that sometimes that which seems to be a setback can end up being for the best. I can only imagine that Timothy was meant to stay on in the life he was living, that he had important work to do there that only he could do."

"But what will happen if we can't find him?" asked Tad.

"You must find him," said Tamburlaine. "There is no other way."

"Can you help us?" said Edith.

Tamburlaine looked hard at her. He seemed to be staring down into her very soul. "Yes," he said finally, "I can help you. But it will be dangerous, and it might not work."

"Tell us!" cried the four Byrams all at once.

"I just wonder if it will be possible," said Tamburlaine, an apprehensive tone creeping into his voice. It was the first time Edith had ever heard him sound uncertain.

"You see," said Tamburlaine, "since we no longer know where to seek Timothy in the past, we must seek him in the present, in his other life. And in the present, he is a very old man in poor health. He must be found—and soon."

"Do you know where he is?" asked Joe.

"No," said Tamburlaine, "no one knows where he is. But I can feel his energy diminishing. He has not long."

"It is up to Edith now," Tamburlaine continued. "She is the one who found the room. Edith may be a channel for Timothy. I only hope it will be enough."

"Tell us!" Martha cried.

"Edith must try to let Timothy reach *her*. Then, once Edith feels his presence, she must concentrate on creating a door. With the ring's help, this door may lead to where Timothy waits."

"What about us?" asked Martha. "Can't we go with Edith?"

"Four people traveling at once would be impossible," said Tamburlaine gently. "Even for one it can be risky."

"If it's that risky, maybe I should go," said Joe.

"No, Joe," said Tamburlaine. "Edith must go. She has the best chance to succeed. And she must go alone. With no specific destination, one slight lapse of concentration and Edith could go almost anywhere."

Joe handed Edith the ring and he, Tad, and Martha formed a circle. Edith closed her eyes and tried to concentrate on Timothy, but it was hard work. She kept thinking of other things: her father, her writing assignment for school, her cousins. But at last she thought she felt Timothy calling to her, a soft voice heard above a strong wind.

As she concentrated, a door appeared in the wall of Tamburlaine's cabin—a dark door. Edith walked to the door and stepped through.

It was empty and awful where Edith went. Dry, baked earth stretched almost to the horizon. A red sun was beating down from a yellow sky. Ghastly hot winds blew dust into her face. Shielding her eyes against the wind and the sun, Edith saw, far distant on the horizon, what looked like a giant glass dome. In it she thought she made out modern-looking buildings and some greenery. It seemed impossibly far away.

I'll never make it there, thought Edith desperately, not in this heat and against this wind. Never!

Looking around her at the baked bleakness, Edith quickly decided that she must have gone to the wrong time and place altogether. But how could she get back?

There was no doorway on this level, vacant plain.

She had no choice. Bending down, she started pawing at the soil. It was horribly warm; it nearly scalded her fingers. Still she kept digging, for she had seen a few charred pieces of wood half buried in the parched earth.

It was hard work. The wind never let up, but it was always changing direction, so whatever dirt Edith dug up invariably blew into her face.

Sweat was pouring off her and her eyes were tearing from the wind and the dust and the dirt. It might have been hours later, but at last she had unearthed three long, thin pieces of wood. Nearby, a dead vine was attached to a piece of barbed wire that was sticking out of the earth. Edith disentangled the vine.

It was almost impossible to work in such a strong wind, but Edith managed to tie the three pieces of wood together, forming a large square U. Turning it upside down, she stuck the ends into the dry earth so the U could stand up on its own. In all the time she'd been struggling, no living thing had passed by, not even an insect.

"I hope this counts as a door!" said Edith as she stepped through the U.

She felt the pull. The heat and the sour wind vanished. Edith whirled through color and light; at once she landed back in Tamburlaine's cabin.

It took only one glance to know Edith had experienced something horrible.

"Where was I?" cried Edith.

"It could be the future," said Tamburlaine. "Or one that may yet be averted. It is impossible to say."

Edith washed her face and shook the sand from her clothing.

"Are you still willing?" asked Tamburlaine. "For now you have seen the risks."

Edith looked at Joe, Tad, and Martha. She could do it for them, if not just for herself. "Yes," she said. "I'm ready."

Again Tad, Martha, and Joe formed a circle. But this time, Tamburlaine led Edith into the room that wasn't there. "The voyage out might be easier from here," Tamburlaine said gently.

He left the door open, so Edith could see back into his cabin, where her cousins stood holding hands in a ring, the owl and the fox watching intently.

A strong wind was blowing through the room, an urgent wind in a great hurry to get somewhere.

It was hard concentrating with the wind raging around her, but Edith tried. At first it seemed impossible, but then, soft against the wind, she heard it. She was sure this time. It was Timothy's voice, calling her from somewhere.

A door appear on the far wall. Edith stepped through.

This time she was in a quiet bedroom. Green light from a garden below filtered through a window.

At first Edith thought she was alone. Then she sensed someone watching her. She wheeled around.

He was sitting in a rocking chair. His eyes and his smile were still the same, but nothing else was. Timothy Byram had gone from being a healthy teenager to a frail old man. White hair crowned a wrinkled face, and his once strong hands were now gnarled.

To Edith's amazement, he didn't seem at all surprised to see her. "Edith," he said, "I've waited for your return, and now you're here. And you're real. You're not a ghost. I am glad to see you again."

"We've been looking for you everywhere," burst out Edith. "Really. But we couldn't find out what happened to you after you were in London."

"London," said Timothy, "that was a long time ago. . . . That boy Joe and his brother and sister ended up saving my life. German bombs leveled the factory where I was staying. But the second they'd pulled me from beneath a fallen beam, why, they just vanished the way you did back at the circus."

"Whatever happened to Evan?" asked Edith. "Joe, Martha, and Tad were wondering."

"I saw him again at Mrs. Bellerby's. He wondered about Joe, Martha, and Tad, too—not that I could tell him much. I just learned recently that he became a well-known playwright. Anyway, as you must have heard from Joe, I was being trained for espionage work in London. I turned out to have a good ear for language. I ended up being sent into Nazi Germany; I was able to infiltrate the upper echelons of their intelligence network. Some say the information I relayed back to the English greatly helped the Allies win the war."

"So you *did* have important work to do," said Edith to herself. "Tamburlaine was right, as usual."

"After the war," continued Timothy, "I retired from espionage. It was considered too dangerous for me to resume my former name, so I was given a new identity, a new name. And I had to choose a new career."

"What did you become?"

"I became a painter," said Timothy, "and to my surprise, I did rather well at it."

"Maybe I've heard of you," said Edith. "In fact, my great-aunt is an artist."

"I am now known as Simon Andrews."

"Simon Andrews!" gasped Edith. "Why, you live right near Rock Ridge!"

"That's why I settled here. I remembered this area so clearly from when I was with Sheehan's Traveling Circus. I was only here briefly but somehow I never forgot this place. So, about ten years ago, I decided to settle here. It's still almost as beautiful as I remember it being back when I was a teenager. In recent years I've become ill and am confined to bed. But at least I can look out my window into the garden, and out to the hills and sky beyond. I sit and dream for hours. Sometimes I dream about the circus, and sometimes I dream about a place with bluebirds flying overhead, and of two girls—one who looks like me."

"Were you lonely here once you became ill?" asked Edith gently.

"It has been a hard few years," admitted Timothy. "You see, Edith, I know I can't get better. But I keep feeling that I have something left to do, something that keeps me going. Yet I don't know what it is. And now it turns out that an artist I've long admired lives nearby in Greenvale, but my health hasn't permitted us to meet."

"That artist in Greenvale," said Edith, "that's my Great-aunt Ruth—Ruth Byram. We met her together once—the day of Mike's funeral.

"Timothy," Edith burst out, "now I can tell you what I

153

never had the chance to before. You know Ruth? Well, she's not only my great-aunt, she's also your sister."

"My sister?"

"She's your baby sister. And I'm your granddaughter."

It didn't take long. Soon Timothy believed Edith.

"My dear!" he cried, embracing Edith with his thin arms.

"Now," said Edith, "if you come with me, I can take you home."

"I'm ready," said Timothy. "I want to go where I belong."

"Can you stand?" asked Edith.

"With a lot of assistance."

"Two yards is about all we need," said Edith, eyeing the distance from the rocking chair to the door.

At last they made it to the door. Edith could hear the housekeeper downstairs preparing tea, but there was no way to explain to her where Timothy was going. She would never believe it.

"Take me home," said Timothy.

Edith put the ring back on, and, grasping both of Timothy's gnarled hands, she guided him through the door.

19
THE FINAL RETURN

The next second they were back in the room that wasn't there.

It was empty except for Tamburlaine. And still, too. The wind had died down entirely. Smiling calmly, Tamburlaine helped Edith steer Timothy toward the door of his cabin.

It seemed to take forever, but at last Edith could see into Tamburlaine's comfortable living room. There stood Joe, Martha, and Tad. And the owl and the fox.

But there was someone else there, too. Someone who looked a lot like Martha.

Edith looked again and smiled.

It was Rosamond.

With a wild, happy shout, she came charging across the room to them.

Edith looked toward the frail, exhausted Timothy and saw him changing before her eyes. The white hair turned gray and then blond; the wrinkles smoothed away altogether; the bent, ailing body of an old man soon was that

155

of a limber, healthy young boy. Timothy now looked the same age as he did when Edith had first met him.

"Timmy!" cried Rosamond.

"Rosie!" answered Timothy. Edith had told him everything, of course; but even if she hadn't, Timothy felt that just seeing Rosamond would have reminded him of all he had forgotten.

The next second, brother and sister were locked in a loving embrace, crying and laughing all at once.

Tamburlaine watched, a contented look on his mysterious face. The owl, too, seemed pleased.

At last Tamburlaine spoke. "Rosamond and Timothy," he said, "it is time for the final return. Rosamond, you will pass through the door first. You will arrive back not at the time you left, however, but at the time when you were a young child. Timothy, you will go second. For you the door will lead back to the time when you were in the hospital in Boston. You will both lose all memory of what has happened here. Indeed, Rosamond, the time spent in the room that wasn't there will cease to exist. And Timothy, your other life will appear merely a dream."

"But how will Timothy return to Bluebird Hall if you send him back to the hospital?" asked Tad. "Good grief, what if they lose him again!"

"He will not be lost this time, I promise. Joe," Tamburlaine continued, "don't you have a bracelet that belonged to your father—a silver bracelet with the name 'Byram' engraved on it?"

"Yes," said Joe. "My dad inherited it from his dad. Then I got it."

"You will have it again," said Tamburlaine. "It just has

to make another circle through time before it returns to you."

Joe removed the bracelet and gave it to Tamburlaine.

Tamburlaine attached it very securely to Timothy's wrist.

Then he directed Rosamond into the room that wasn't there. "You shall return through the door by which you came," Tamburlaine told her.

With a wave and a smile, Rosamond headed toward the door at the far end.

Edith, Joe, Tad, and Martha stood together to watch her go. At first they thought the room must have become amazingly long. Rosamond appeared so far distant as she moved off that they felt as if they were looking at someone much farther away.

Edith was the first to realize it wasn't that Rosamond was so far off, it was that she was turning back into a three year old. Indeed, when she arrived at the door, she couldn't reach the doorknob. But a sudden gust of wind blew the door open for her. The little girl stepped through and was gone.

The door seemed to shut of its own accord and then disappear.

Timothy was next. He shook Tamburlaine's hand, then hugged Tad, Martha, and Joe all together. Then he hugged Edith.

"I always wanted to meet my grandfather," said Tad. "And now I have, and he looks just like my brother Joe!"

"I even remember you," Joe told Timothy, "as an old, old man."

"Then," said Timothy, "we shall meet again."

Timothy took another look at Edith, Tad, Martha, and Joe. Then he smiled and said, "I am proud to have such wonderful grandchildren." Then he turned and approached a door that had appeared in the wall of Tamburlaine's cabin—a hospital door.

Edith thought she must have blinked. Tad, Martha, and Joe thought the same thing.

"It must have been a long blink," said Martha afterward, because when they looked next, they saw Tamburlaine carrying Timothy. And Timothy was just a small child. He was wrapped in a white blanket, and his little face was flushed with fever.

The door flew open as Tamburlaine approached it.

Peering through the door, the four cousins saw long, white corridors. It was, Edith knew, the hospital in Boston.

Leaning through the open door, Tamburlaine gently placed Timothy on a broad table.

As the door shut slowly, they caught a quick glimpse of a nurse hurrying along, her shoes clipping along the corridor.

"Ah," she said, picking up Timothy. "Here's the Byram boy. Goodness! We've been calling him by another name! Somehow I never noticed this bracelet until now," she added, just as the door shut tight.

"Timothy is returned to his proper place," said Tamburlaine. "The strand is rewoven into the fabric. All is well, then and now."

"Then why do I feel so sad?" asked Edith.

"You and Timothy became friends," Tamburlaine said.

"Friends who went through much together. It is only natural that you should miss him when he goes. But I would say that you have found other friends, haven't you?"

Edith looked shyly at her cousins. They smiled back at her.

"You're not just a cousin," said Joe, "you're a friend—a good friend."

"Tamburlaine," began Tad, his scientific glow lighting his brown eyes, "what will happen to all the things Timothy made and did in his other life? Will it all just vanish?"

"No," replied Tamburlaine, "all the good he did and all the art he created in his other life will remain on in this life. In fact, there will be those who will actually remember him. In a sense, Timothy can be said to have led dual lives."

"That's good," said Martha, "otherwise all the people who owned his paintings would be pretty upset to find the frames empty!"

"Now," said Tamburlaine, "I have something for you. Come and see."

Tamburlaine led them out of his house and into the room that wasn't there. This time a beckoning wind wafted through it, a wind rich with the smell of autumn bonfires. Tamburlaine nodded toward the far wall, now blank since the door through which Rosamond had come and gone had vanished.

The Byrams watched a new door appear on the wall.

As Tamburlaine led them toward it, it opened and the smell of burning leaves grew stronger.

"You may enter," he said.

In the present it was the junk room. Now it seemed to be a small sitting room. Looking out the window, the four Byrams saw it was a crisp autumn afternoon, the ground thick with fallen leaves.

"What year is it?" Tad wanted to know, but Tamburlaine just nodded toward the window.

On the lawn beneath them stood a man and two boys. The man was raking leaves, but the moment he raked some into a good pile, the boys would leap on it and scatter the leaves merrily.

"That's Timothy!" gasped Joe.

"Then those boys must be his sons," said Tad.

"That's our dad!" cried Martha.

"And that's my dad with him," said Edith, starting to cry, but mostly from happiness. "I always wanted to see him again."

For several long minutes they watched the man and the two boys laughing and playing in the autumn leaves.

Then the boys ran off and their father ran after them. They ran out of sight. Soon all that Edith, Tad, Martha, and Joe could hear were their happy cries, then those, too, faded into the bright air.

"It is time to go," said Tamburlaine, ushering the four Byrams back into the room that wasn't there.

"We, too, must part," said Tamburlaine simply. "Our task is completed. It is time."

Somehow Edith knew she had to relinquish the ring.

"But, Tamburlaine," cried Martha, "will we ever get to use the ring again?"

"It is up to the ring," said Tamburlaine. "Perhaps it will find you. It has before, you know. Twice."

160

"And you, Tamburlaine," said Edith. "Will we ever find you again?"

Somehow she knew that once they left the room this time, it really would become the room that wasn't there.

"Time will tell," said Tamburlaine. "I can only say that there is no use in looking for magic; magic has to find you. Now it is time to go."

It was hard saying good-bye to Tamburlaine. Even the owl looked a bit misty-eyed as farewells were being said.

"You have done well," said Tamburlaine, hugging the four Byrams. "You have all done very well."

Edith, Tad, Martha, and Joe stepped through the door into Edith's bedroom. Looking behind them, they saw the room vanish into darkness, its place taken by a white plaster wall.

It was the following Saturday.

In the meantime, they'd had many conversations with Mrs. Byram about their Grandfather Timothy and their Great-aunt Rosamond. "Why this sudden interest?" Mrs. Byram had inquired, but received no real answer. Edith, Tad, Martha, and Joe soon learned that Timothy Byram had indeed been sent to a hospital in Boston when he wasn't yet four years old.

"It was a lucky thing they were so honest at that hospital," Mrs. Byram remarked.

"What do you mean?" asked Martha.

"You know that silver bracelet Joe inherited from his dad?" asked Mrs. Byram. "Well, his dad inherited it from his dad. Somehow, when Grandfather Timothy was sent to the hospital, they forgot to take it off. Ruth says that

161

her mother always claimed she specifically remembered taking it off and putting it in the cupboard for safekeeping, but I suppose in her concern she just *thought* she had. In any case, no one took it. Aren't you glad, Joe?" she asked. "I know how fond you are of it."

Joe colored slightly. He hadn't seen the bracelet since Tamburlaine had put it on his grandfather's wrist.

"Have you shown it to Edith?" asked Mrs. Byram.

"I've already—" began Edith, but Mrs. Byram kept on talking.

"Joe always wears it," she said. "Take a look," she added, suddenly reaching over to touch the cuff of Joe's shirt.

"Don't, Mom!" cried Joe, but it was too late.

How'll I ever explain this? he was wondering when his mother spoke.

"It *is* handsome," she said, "a real family heirloom."

Joe looked down.

The bracelet had returned.

Too soon a tan Chevrolet made its way down Bluebird Hall's driveway. It was Aunt Alida, there to pick up Edith and spend the night before returning to New York.

"Edith," she said, "you look wonderful."

Edith was still wearing her hair up the way Rosamond did. Aunt Alida had also been pleased to learn that Edith's writing project had been sent off in time.

"A good thing it was," she said. "It is, after all, extremely important."

Upon hearing this, Mrs. Byram arched an eyebrow and began practicing the speech she'd vowed to give her sister-in-law.

"After lunch," she told herself. "I'll do it after lunch."

"Have you heard the latest news?" Mrs. Byram asked over lunch. "It's quite a mystery. Do you recall Great-aunt Ruth mentioning that painter she admired, the one who was so ill? Well, it seems he disappeared, and they say he's been bedridden for years."

"But that's impossible," said Aunt Alida.

"The housekeeper says that she heard voices from his bedroom. It sounded as though he were talking to a young girl. But when she went to see, the door was open and the room was empty. The police have searched, but no trace of him has been found."

"Or ever will," said Martha.

"What did you say, dear?"

"I said, 'I'm sure they will'—find a trace, I mean."

"Well, I'm sure Ruth will be terribly upset. In fact, she should be here any minute."

Lunch was over and the dishes were being cleared when Mrs. Byram took Aunt Alida aside.

"Alida," she began when she heard Martha calling from the front door. "It's a registered letter for Edith," she called.

"For me? Who would be sending me a registered letter?" asked Edith, drying off her hands at the sink.

"It's from your school," replied Martha, reading the return address.

"Open it, Edith," urged Joe.

With her mother watching nervously, Edith opened the envelope and read the letter.

She looked astonished.

"I don't get it," she said finally. "I sent in the piece I

wrote, to see if I could get in that special writing class, and they've written back to say I've received a full scholarship. There must be some mistake. I never applied for any scholarship."

"I guess it's time for me to confess," said Aunt Alida. "You see, Edith, you *were* applying for a scholarship when you wrote that piece."

"But why didn't you tell me?"

"Edith, dear, I didn't want you to worry. I was afraid I wouldn't be able to pay for your new school. And I didn't want the weight of that on your shoulders. I thought just writing the paper would be pressure enough."

"I wish you had told me, Mom!"

"Perhaps I should have. But I knew you'd do your best on the paper no matter why you were writing it, so I didn't worry about the quality of your work. I just wanted you to have as good a time as possible with your cousins here at Bluebird Hall—a place your father loved so."

"Hey, Edith," said Joe, "what did you end up writing about?"

"It was a story," said Edith, "about a girl who traveled through time and joined a circus."

"Did someone mention a circus?" asked a voice from the kitchen door.

It was Great-aunt Ruth with a package in her hand.

"Yes, Ruth," said Mrs. Byram. "Edith just wrote a story about a circus that won her a scholarship."

"How grand," said Great-aunt Ruth. "They do say writing about one's own experiences is a good way to start."

"What do you have there?" asked Mrs. Byram.

"It's the painting Simon Andrews sent to me. It's just arrived."

"I suppose you've heard—" began Mrs. Byram.

"Yes, I have," interrupted Great-aunt Ruth. "And somehow I'm not worried. I have the feeling that he simply went, well, that he went home."

"You are such a mystery sometimes, Ruth," said Mrs. Byram. "And speaking of mysteries, remember that photograph you took of Tad, Martha, and Joe—the one that was fading? Well, I just took a look at it, and it's completely back to normal. I simply cannot understand it."

"Some things *are* hard to understand," replied Ruth. Was it Edith's imagination, or had Ruth winked at her as she was speaking?

Tad, Martha, and Joe smiled to think of the photograph. The two photographs Ruth had given them of themselves and the one Edith had taken of herself were now good as new. The second they'd returned from their last visit to Tamburlaine they'd checked them. Finding their own images clear and unfaded was the final proof that their mission had been successful.

"Well, come on, Ruth," said Mrs. Byram, "show us the painting."

"Here it is," said Ruth, propping the picture up on the kitchen table. "And quite a coincidence it is, too. Remember my first photo, the one of the circus ticket booth?"

"Actually, no, the children never got around to showing it to me."

"Well, this painting complements it perfectly. It's entitled *The Haunted Circus—Greenvale, 1923.*"

"My, but it's lovely!" exclaimed Mrs. Byram as they all crowded around to look. "It's such a bright, sunny circus. I wonder why it's titled *The Haunted Circus?*"

Aunt Alida spotted it first. "My word," she said, "look over here. This girl here, with the owl on her shoulder—she looks just like Edith!"

"And look over here," cried Mrs. Byram, "at this group of three children. They look just like Tad, Martha, and Joe!"

"Quite a coincidence, I should say," remarked Great-aunt Ruth.

The two sisters-in-law took the painting into the living room where the light was better, still marveling at the amazing coincidence.

"I must be seeing things," they heard Aunt Alida say from the living room, "or else my memory's a bit off, but I could swear the portrait of Timothy Byram has changed expressions. Look, he's smiling. I recall his expression as being rather stern."

"I don't think so," they heard Mrs. Byram reply. "Maybe it's the angle."

"I just thought of something," said Edith to Tad, Martha, and Joe. "I think I know why that painting's called *The Haunted Circus.*"

"Because of the fake ghosts at Sheehan's Circus?" said Joe.

"No," said Edith, "I think to Simon Andrews, *we* must have seemed like ghosts, always showing up again and disappearing into thin air—"

166

"And never getting older or changing," added Martha.

"But Martha and I weren't at the circus," pointed out Tad.

"That must be why he put you two off on one side, behind that gray smoke. Maybe he was putting a little of his memories of London into the circus painting."

"So," said Joe, "we were his own private ghosts."

"That's about right," said a voice behind them. It was Great-aunt Ruth. They hadn't noticed she'd stayed with them in the kitchen. "You know," she continued, "I've always thought that Edith reminded me of someone. I didn't figure out who it was until the other day when I saw her in those old-fashioned clothes. Then it all came back to me. I remembered this strange dream I'd had—a dream that seemed so real—of my brother vanishing and Rosamond being sent off to boarding school, and of almost losing Bluebird Hall, and of a girl coming from far away to help."

"Then you know?" began Edith.

"Timothy, too, always had such strange dreams," continued Great-aunt Ruth. "He would tell them to me. They were about a circus, and there was also this recurring dream about being older and in a gray city that was being bombed. And there was another dream of being old and ill and alone, and of being rescued by a blue-eyed girl. There were always children in his dreams, children who would help him—even save his life."

"Did he tell you their names?" asked Tad.

Great-aunt Ruth just gave an enigmatic smile.

"So you do know!" cried Edith.

"I do now," said Great-aunt Ruth, "and I want to thank you. I think you know for what. Oh," she continued, "I almost forgot. I have one for each of you."

"Where did you get these?" asked Martha.

"That would be a long story," said Great-aunt Ruth with a twinkle in her eye. "A very long story."

For what Ruth had given each of them was a feather from Tamburlaine's owl—a beautiful moon-white, magic-looking feather.

"And," continued Ruth, "I have a message for you, or more precisely, a reminder."

"What is it?" asked Martha excitedly.

The four cousins had drawn closer together to hear the answer. Their arms were around each other's shoulders as they leaned closer to listen.

"I am to tell you," said Great-aunt Ruth, "that there is no use looking for magic . . ."

A sigh of disappointment from Martha was interrupted by the end of the sentence.

". . . because magic has to find you. And something tells me it will."